PURRFECT SON

THE MYSTERIES OF MAX 27

NIC SAINT

PUSS IN PRINT PUBLICATIONS

PURRFECT SON

The Mysteries of Max 27

Copyright © 2020 by Nic Saint

All rights reserved. No part of this book may be reproduced in any form by any electronic or mechanical means including photocopying, recording, or information storage and retrieval without permission in writing from the author.

This is a work of fiction. Names, characters, places, brands, media, and incidents are either the product of the author's imagination or are used fictitiously. The author acknowledges the trademarked status and trademark owners of various products referenced in this work of fiction, which have been used without permission. The publication/use of these trademarks is not authorized, associated with, or sponsored by the trademark owners.

Edited by Chereese Graves

www.nicsaint.com

Give feedback on the book at: info@nicsaint.com

facebook.com/nicsaintauthor
@nicsaintauthor

First Edition

Printed in the U.S.A

1

Marge had recently bought herself a new couch to replace the one she'd used for the past fifteen years, and of course it hadn't taken long for us cats to explore its many advantages, such as there were: softness, firmness, and the many other characteristics that potentially turned it into our new favorite spot to lounge on and take those precious catnaps that we enjoy so much.

Marge had, of course, put down a blanket to prevent us from ruining her new couch—as if we could ever ruin a couch simply by our mere presence—and when we'd communicated our disfavor of the new blanket, she'd put down a protective sheet. All in all I think we'd used the couch more than she or Tex ever had, or Gran, and I don't think that was exactly what she'd had in mind at the time of purchase.

Then again, if you're going to be a cat lady, you have to be prepared for the consequences is what I always say.

And so it was that four cats were lounging happily on Marge's new acquisition, sleeping peacefully and generally spending a lazy morning at home.

Marge was at the library, Tex was at the doctor's office, and so was Gran, and next door the house was empty, too, as Odelia had gone to work, and so had her boyfriend.

I have to admit I thoroughly enjoy these lazy mornings, when the house is quiet and it's just us cats, with no humans to disturb us or to trouble us with their dramas.

"Max?" suddenly asked Dooley, rousing me from my slumber.

"Mh?" I said with some reluctance, for I'd just been dreaming of the largest and tastiest chicken nugget I'd ever encountered. That chicken nugget was mine, and now it simply vanished as I opened my eyes. Bummer.

"Do you hear that?" he asked.

I noticed how my friend had tensed up, and he looked as much like a pointing dog as a pointing dog could look if he were a smallish gray cat.

Dooley has these moments when he starts seeing things that aren't really there, like mysterious diseases that suddenly afflict him, or the sky falling on top of our heads when the sky is still firmly attached to whatever the sky is attached to.

But this time I had to admit he wasn't hallucinating, or getting all worked up for no reason whatsoever. There was indeed a noise where no noise should have been. It sounded like… scratching.

"Do you think it's burglars?" asked Dooley, eyes wide and fearful.

"I hope it's not mice," said Harriet, who'd also woken up.

"Or rats," grunted Brutus, located right next to his girlfriend.

I pricked up my ears a little more, and surmised that the sound seemed to emanate from upstairs, which was of course quite impossible, as the house was empty.

"It seems to come from upstairs," now also determined Harriet, whose hearing is on par with that of the rest of us.

"Let's go and have a look," said Brutus with a yawn, and made to get up.

"Are you crazy?" said Harriet. "For all we know it could be burglars, like Dooley says, and then where would that leave us?"

"Um, heroes when we catch these burglars?"

"Yeah, dead heroes," said Harriet. "I say we stay right here and pretend we didn't hear a thing."

"How can we pretend not to hear a thing when burglars are cleaning out the house?" said Brutus. It's at times like these that you can see that Brutus used to belong to Chase before ownership was transferred to the Poole family. He still thinks like a cop's cat.

"Look, it can't hurt to take a little look-see," I said now. "We simply sneak up on the burglars and then we sneak away again and go and warn our humans. Easy-peasy."

"I don't know," said Harriet doubtfully. "I'm too young to die, you guys."

"Nobody's going to die," I said. "We'll just pop upstairs and then pop down again—no harm done."

"All of us?" Brutus grunted. "I think we should probably send one cat up there to check—doesn't seem right for all of us to risk our lives."

"Brutus is right," said Harriet. "If we all go we're going to attract a lot of unwanted attention for sure. So who's volunteering for the mission? Please raise your paw."

I glanced around, and when I didn't see any paws going up, not even Brutus's, I decided to stick mine up. I mean, I'm not the bravest cat in the world—anything but—but when it comes to protecting my turf I can usually be relied upon to go the extra mile.

"I'll come, too," said Brutus.

"And me," said Dooley.

"Oh, maybe I'll join you guys," said Harriet with an

eyeroll. "It just wouldn't feel right for me to stay behind while you all go into battle," she explained.

And so it was decided: we'd all go in search of this intrepid intruder, and make sure we got his or her features committed to memory so we could offer our humans a nice description.

And as one cat, we all slid down from our new favorite couch, and set paw for the staircase. And we'd just reached the bottom of the stairs when the curious sounds intensified.

"That's clearly not a mouse," said Harriet.

"Or a rat," grunted Brutus.

"Oh, you guys," said Dooley with a slight whimper. "I'm getting really scared now."

"Don't be scared, Dooley," I said. "We're cats. Whoever these intruders are, we can easily outrun them—if they even happen to notice us in the first place."

Humans, as a rule, usually fail to pay attention to pets wandering about the home—and that goes double for intruders, who watch out for dogs, and neglect to see the danger in cats—at their own peril, I might add.

So we all snuck up the stairs, not making a single sound, listening carefully all the while. The sound seemed to come from... the attic. And once we were upstairs, I saw that indeed the attic ladder had been pulled down, and it now became clear to me that someone was rummaging around up there.

"Who wants to go first?" asked Harriet, as she darted nervous glances at the hole in the ceiling that led up to the attic.

"I'll go," I said with a shrug. "I don't mind." I'd already figured out how this was going to go down, too: I'd simply sneak up that ladder, and then take a quick peek around the attic and see what was going on. I wasn't entirely without a sense of approaching danger, but frankly my curiosity trumped my sense of self-preservation at that moment, behavior I've been told is typical for cats.

"I'll be right behind you," said Brutus, who didn't want to look weak in front of his lady.

"And me," said Dooley, whose curiosity seemed to have been piqued, too.

"And me," said Harriet after a moment's hesitation.

And so it was decided: I carefully navigated that folding wooden ladder first, then Brutus, then Dooley, and finally Harriet brought up the rear.

And as I raised my head and took a peek, I saw that a person wearing a motorcycle helmet was opening and closing drawers in a dresser located on the other side of the attic. The person looked pretty buff, and was dressed in a black leather jacket, black jeans and heavy work boots. He looked like a man to me, and definitely not a member of the Poole family.

"What do you see?" asked Brutus.

"A man!" I whispered. "He's opening and closing drawers!"

"What's going on?" asked Harriet from lower on the ladder.

"Max says that it's a man!" Brutus loud-whispered.

"It's a man!" said Dooley, sounding panicky.

"A man!" Harriet cried. "What man?"

"Harriet is asking for the man!" said Dooley.

"Harriet wants to know about that man!" Brutus said.

"You don't have to shout!" I said. "I can hear Harriet perfectly fine. He's wearing a motorcycle helmet, so I can't see his face."

"He's wearing a motorcycle helmet so Max can't see his face!" said Brutus.

"Max is wearing a motorcycle helmet so he can't see the man's face!" Dooley translated the message.

"Why is Max wearing a motorcycle helmet?" asked Harriet, confused.

The man, meanwhile, must have become aware that he was being watched, for he now looked up, and I saw that he was staring intently in my direction. I ducked down. It's never a fun prospect to be attacked by a man wearing a motorcycle helmet. And this motorcycle man looked like he might very well eat cats for breakfast—literally!

"Lemme see," now said Harriet, and shoved Dooley aside, then squeezed past Brutus, and finally joined me on the top step.

"I think he saw me!" I said. "He was looking straight at me just now."

"Oh, nonsense," said Harriet. "Humans never pay attention to cats." And with these words, she popped her head up. Moments later, she popped down again. "Max?" she said.

"Yes?"

"I think you're right. I think he saw us."

"And what makes you say that?"

"Because he's right here, staring at me!"

And as I slowly glanced up, I saw that Harriet wasn't lying: the man was now face to face with me, and so I yelped in fear.

"Cats!" the man growled, not sounding all that fond of our species. "I should have known."

And with these words, he grabbed both me and Harriet by the scruff of our necks, and hoisted us up and into the attic proper, then proceeded to carry us away.

Now I know I should have put up a fight at this point, but I was so startled by this unexpected development that the thought didn't even cross my mind, and clearly it didn't cross Harriet's mind either!

And so before we knew it, we suddenly found ourselves

thrown into a large chest, and when the lid slammed down on top of us, I suddenly realized our predicament.

"Max!" Harriet cried as darkness descended upon us. "He caught us!"

And when suddenly the chest was opened once more and two more cats were deposited inside, it was clear that our strategy had backfired to a substantial degree.

We were, for all intents and purposes, in quite the pickle!

2

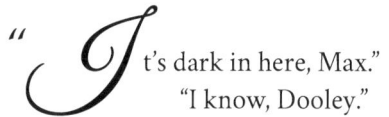

"It's dark in here, Max."
"I know, Dooley."
"I don't like it."
"Me neither."

"Oh, could you please stop talking, the both of you," said Harriet. "I'm trying to figure out a way to get us out of here and all this babble is making it hard for me to think."

"Why don't we simply put our backs into it?" Brutus suggested. "I mean, the lid on this thing can't be that heavy, can it?"

"Good idea, snuggle bear," said Harriet. "Max, Dooley, up," she instructed, our unexpected captivity making her a little more snappish than usual.

So Dooley and I dutifully did as we were told and arched our backs so we could raise the lid on our makeshift prison. Unfortunately the thing didn't budge. Not even an inch.

"I think he locked it," I said.

"How do you know it was a he, Max?" asked Dooley. "Couldn't it have been a she?"

"It could have been a she," I allowed. After all, it was hard to make out who our assailant was underneath that motorcycle helmet.

"So now what, Brutus?" asked Harriet, who was still focused on the task at hand, and much to her credit, too, I might add.

"Now we wait," Brutus suggested.

"Wait for what? Santa Claus?"

"Now we wait for someone to come and save us," he said. "Sooner or later Marge or Gran or Odelia will realize we've gone missing, and that's when they'll come looking."

"They'll never find us in here," said Harriet, offering the pessimistic view. "Unless…"

I could almost hear her brain working—it was even starting to radiate heat as it did.

"It's getting very hot in here," announced Dooley, who'd noticed the same thing.

"That's because this is a very small space and we're four cats in here," I said, not wanting to cast aspersions on Harriet's brain.

"No, but it's getting very, very hot in here," my friend said.

And I have to admit that he was right. It was getting extremely hot in that chest.

And then I saw it: a glow was lighting up our new unfavorite spot, to such an extent it couldn't possibly be caused by Harriet's brain. She's a smart cat, but not that smart.

"We're on fire!" suddenly Harriet cried out. "The attic must be on fire!"

"Oh, no!" cried Dooley. "I don't like fire. Fires are very dangerous. The Discovery Channel warns against fires all the time! Fires, like, kill things."

I swallowed a little. This wasn't good. I mean, the likes of Houdini would probably have uttered a careless little laugh at a predicament such as the one we now found ourselves in: he'd even have added a few more obstacles to make it really interesting. Like shackles. Or a harness. But for me this was already more than bad enough, to be honest!

"Oh, Max, we're going to die," Dooley announced. He gulped a little, then said, "I think you guys are the best friends a cat could ever have had the pleasure to meet, and I want you to know that it's been an honor. And a pleasure. In fact an honor and a pleasure."

"Oh, Dooley, shut up for a second, will you?" said Harriet. "Maybe this fire is the best thing that could have happened to us. This chest is made of wood, right? And what is one of the basic characteristics of wood?"

"That it feels nice and warm under the paws, especially in the wintertime?" Brutus suggested.

"That it burns!"

"Oh, right. Of course." He paused, then: "So, um, how does that help us?"

"This fire is going to burn right through this wood in the next couple of minutes, and when that happens, we should be ready."

"Ready for what?"

"Ready to die!" said Dooley. "I have a confession to make. Last month, I accidentally peed in your litter box, Brutus. I was in a hurry and I accidentally went into your box by mistake. And by the time I realized, I'd already tinkled in your litter box. Can you ever forgive me?"

"Look, let's all focus for a moment," I said. "Harriet made a very valid point: wood burns, and so this fire is going to eat through this chest soon, and when it does we have to be ready to make a run for it."

"But if the chest is on fire, won't the entire attic be on fire?" Brutus said. "And isn't that going to make it a little hard to make a run for it? My paws are not made of Teflon, you know."

"And then two weeks ago I accidentally did number two

in *your* litter box, Harriet," Dooley continued his timely confession. "I couldn't hold it up long enough to reach my own so I went into yours instead! I'm so sorry!"

"We don't know what the situation is outside of this chest," said Harriet. "But we have to stay positive and hope for the best."

"When people are faced with a big fire like this, they sometimes douse themselves in water," said Brutus. "Pity we don't have a bucket of water at our disposal now."

"No, but we do have something else," said Harriet.

"What's that?" I asked, intrigued what could possibly replace a convenient bucket of water.

And then she spat me in the face!

"Hey, what did you do that for?" I asked, horrified.

But instead of responding, she simply did it again!

"Cut it out, Harriet!" I cried. Getting burned to a crisp is bad enough without being spat on, I mean to say.

"But don't you see, Max!" she cried. "We don't have water but we have our saliva!"

"Brilliant!" said Brutus. "We simply lick ourselves until we're well and truly soaked and by the time that fire eats through this chest, we'll be ready to face the inferno!"

I didn't want to rain on their parade—or even spit—but I still felt I needed to say something. "By the time that fire burns down this chest, it's going to get so hot in here we're going to expire from the sheer heat, not to mention smoke inhalation, and besides, a little bit of spittle isn't going to protect us from those flames. Only a heat-resistant suit like firemen like to wear is going to accomplish that."

"Oh, why always with all the negatives, Max!" said Harriet. "I'm trying to stay positive here, you know."

"All right, all right," I said, trying to think of something positive to add to the conversation.

"And then last week I accidentally peed in your water bowl, Max," said Dooley now. "It was an accident, I swear!"

"Oh, Dooley," said Harriet with a sigh.

That orange glow that had been getting stronger, and that heat that had been intensifying, told us that the moment had finally come. Our do or die moment, if you will. We'd all been busy licking ourselves, just in case it made a difference, and I have to say my nice blorange coat of fur was pretty slick by now.

The flames were crackling, and Harriet said, "This is it. The moment of truth!"

"The truth is it just happened," Dooley said. "I guess I was still sleepy from my nap. I saw the bowl, and the next moment I was taking a tinkle, even before I realized it wasn't my litter box. And I meant to tell you, Max, I really did, but then I forgot. I'm so, so sorry!"

"This is it, folks!" said Harriet. "Get ready to run!"

The wood creaked and groaned, and I tensed all my muscles, ready to make a desperate run for it, when suddenly there was a loud swooshing sound, then voices could be heard, and the next moment the chest was opened and the face of Chase Kingsley appeared, followed by the face of Odelia, our very own human!

"Am I dreaming?" asked Dooley. "Or did I die and go to heaven?"

3

"I don't get it," said Chase, as he looked around the attic at the devastation. "If they wanted to burn the house down wouldn't they have set fire to other parts of the house?"

Odelia, who'd been hugging her cats, nodded. "I think this was a targeted attack."

"An attack on what?"

She was reluctant to say it out loud in front of her fur babies, who'd already been through a great ordeal, but it was important that they, too, realized what was going on here. "I think the culprit wanted to set fire to... our cats," she said finally.

Max looked up at this. He'd been inspecting their makeshift prison for the past five minutes, and nodded sagely at these words. "He specifically set fire to this wooden chest," he said. "Or trunk, or whatever you call this thing."

"It used to belong to my dad," said Odelia. "And to his dad before him. Dad used it when he was in college. It contained all of his stuff and he kept it in his dorm all those years before shipping it back here."

The only part of the attic that had burned was that particular chest belonging to her dad, and it stood to reason that the attacker must have used some kind of accelerant or maybe even simple lighter fluid to make sure the chest would burn well.

"But why would anyone target the cats?" asked Chase.

"He was snooping around over there," said Max, pointing to an old dresser in the corner of the attic. "He was opening and closing the drawers, and seemed to be looking for something. And then when he caught us spying on him, he didn't seem surprised. He said, 'Cats! I should have known.' As if he was expecting us."

"And then he caught us and locked us up and set us on fire," said Brutus, summing up the state of affairs to a T.

Odelia set Dooley down on the floor and walked over to the dresser Max had indicated. She opened the top drawer, and saw that it contained photo albums belonging to her mom and dad. She picked one up and leafed through it. The photos were all familiar: Mom and Dad in their younger years, trekking through Europe, and seeing the sights. A second album contained their wedding photos, and showed them happy and excited to finally tie the knot. Odelia smiled, and wondered why anyone would be interested in these particular photos. And why anyone would want to set her cats on fire.

"Your uncle is here," said Chase as he glanced down the attic ladder.

The shuffling of feet could be heard, and the next moment the head of her uncle Alec cleared the attic opening. He was panting slightly from the exertion. "So what's the verdict?" he asked as he took a breather.

"Looks like we've got ourselves a burglar who dabbles in animal cruelty," said Chase, and told the chief in a few words what had transpired.

"If we hadn't shown up when we did, my cats would have died," said Odelia.

She tried to hide her distress, but it mustn't have worked well, for Uncle Alec walked over and gave her a comforting pat on the back. "We'll get the bastard, honey. Just you wait and see. And then we'll throw the book at him."

"How did you get here?" asked Max now. "I thought you were both at work?"

"We were," said Odelia. "But Mom called and said she thought she'd left the stove on and asked me to come and check."

"Happens to me all the time," said Uncle Alec. "Sometimes I have to go back twice, just to be sure. Must be old age."

"Or just having a lot of things on your mind," said Odelia.

"I was passing Odelia's office when I saw her walking out," said Chase. "And since criminals have been taking it easy lately, I just figured I'd join her and have an early lunch at the house. Beats the police station canteen."

"So it's actually Marge we have to thank for saving our lives," said Harriet.

"Yeah, I guess it is," said Odelia with a smile. "If she hadn't called…" She didn't want to finish the sentence, or the thought, as it was too horrible to contemplate.

"Harriet had a solution," said Max. "So I like to think we would have made it out safe and sound, even if you hadn't shown up when you did."

It didn't look to Odelia as if Harriet's solution would have done much to alleviate the danger that flaming chest had posed, but this time she decided to keep her tongue.

"The important thing is that you made it out alive," she said. "And maybe," she added with a glance at her boyfriend, "we should keep an eye on you guys from now on. At least until this maniac is caught."

Chase nodded, though she could tell that arranging a

bodyguard for her cats wasn't exactly the solution he'd had in mind for this new situation.

"I'll see if I can't install some kind of an alarm system," said the cop now. "Cameras and stuff, so that if this guy comes back, God forbid, we can catch him in the act."

"I really thought I was going to die," said Dooley now. "And so I said some things that maybe I shouldn't have said."

"What kind of things?" asked Odelia as she crouched down next to the Ragamuffin.

"Like… that I accidentally did wee-wee in Brutus's litter box, and doo-doo in Harriet's litter box, and that I even did wee-wee in Max's water bowl."

She had to suppress a grin, but patted the cat on the head instead. "I don't think your friends will hold it against you, Dooley," she said. "If I had to count the number of times I used Mom and Dad's bathroom instead of my own, I would need more than ten fingers."

"Yes, but for humans it's different," he said. "You only have one bathroom in the house and you all use it. We like to use our own bathroom, and not share it with others."

"It's fine," she said. "I'm sure Harriet and Brutus don't mind if you use their litter box from time to time."

"And Max?" He darted a surreptitious glance at his friend. "Won't he be mad at me?"

"Why don't we ask him? Max!" she called out. "Come over here a minute, will you?"

Dooley gave his friend a worried look.

"What is it?" asked Max.

"Dooley is worried that you're angry with him now that he confessed his little… accident."

Max smiled. "I'd completely forgotten about that already."

"So you aren't mad at me, Max?" asked Dooley.

Max shrugged. "It can happen to the best of us, Dooley.

You're sleepy, stumbling around in the dark, and so you do your business... elsewhere. It's totally fine."

"But... it's not hygienic, Max," Dooley insisted, apparently a glutton for punishment.

Max winced a little at the thought that he'd actually drunk water with a little... extra. "It's okay. I'm still here, aren't I? So clearly drinking that water didn't have any adverse effect on me."

Dooley nodded, but didn't look totally convinced. "I won't do it again, Max, if that's what you're thinking."

"I'm just thinking that I'd like to know who locked us up in that chest."

"Yeah, there's that," said Dooley softly. Oddly enough the peeing incident seemed to be troubling him more than the being-set-on-fire incident. Then again, every cat has his or her hang-ups, and clearly Dooley's hang-up was losing the respect and affection of his peers, and Odelia could absolutely relate with that.

Suddenly there was a loud rumbling on the attic ladder, an anguished cry, and then Mom appeared, followed by Dad and Gran, in that order, and even... Charlene Butterwick, Mayor of Hampton Cove and Uncle Alec's girlfriend.

And so the Poole family was now complete, and as Charlene looked from the burned-out chest to the four cats seated in front of it, she said, "Oh, the poor darlings!"

"It's fine," said Max with a reassuring smile.

"Yeah, we survived," said Harriet with a nod.

"We were saved by Odelia and Chase," intimated Brutus.

"And I'll never pee in Max's bowl again," promised Dooley.

Charlene stared at the cats and uttered a startled laugh. "I keep telling myself that this is impossible—that no cats can talk to their humans—but then I see these guys and..." She shook her head. "At least they're safe. That's the main thing."

4

It was really weird for Charlene to watch Odelia, her mom and her grandma talk to their cats. She watched on, wide-eyed and with not a small sense of wonder, and when her boyfriend sidled up to her and asked, a little worriedly, "Everything all right?" she nodded wordlessly, then went on studying the interactions between man and beast, or, as in this case, woman and beast, feeling as if she'd suddenly landed in a Disney movie.

"Has it always been like this?" she asked. "I mean, has your sister always been able to talk to her cats, or…"

"Or did my mother drop her on her head as a baby and suddenly she became Chatty Cat Cathy? No, she's always been like this," said Alec with a smile. "Unfortunately only the women in our family have the gift."

"Oh. So you don't…"

"No, I don't talk to cats, or dogs, or any other pets."

She flashed him a quick smile. "I'm sorry, Alec. This is all pretty new for me, so…."

He scratched his scalp. "Yeah, I can imagine. That's why I

didn't want to tell you at first. I was afraid you'd freak out and—"

"Run for the hills?"

"Something like that."

"Well, I'm still here, aren't I? Though I have to admit it's going to take some getting used to." She studied the fat orange cat named Max for a moment. He was busy chatting with his human, and Charlene shook her head. "How does it work, exactly? I mean, to me it just sounds like he's meowing, but to Odelia it all makes sense somehow?"

"Yeah, I don't know how it works," said Alec with a shrug. "I just know it does."

"No, but I mean, something inside her brain must be able to compute the sounds her cats make, right? Have you ever had it looked at? By a doctor or a brain specialist or something?" Or a linguist, she wanted to add, then realized that no specialist would be able to figure this out even if they'd believe it in the first place. She hardly believed it herself, still harboring the faint suspicion the entire Poole family was simply performing some kind of elaborate joke at her expense. But since that was even more ridiculous than the simple truth, she placed a hand on Alec's arm and said, "It's just a little weird, is all."

"I know it is, honey," said her big teddy bear of a police chief. "But trust me, you'll get used to it."

"Yeah, I guess I will."

She finally dragged her eyes away from the strange spectacle, and said, "So do you have any idea who did this?"

"Not yet," said Alec, a resolute look stealing over his face, the policeman replacing the boyfriend for a moment. "I've got officers canvassing the neighborhood as we speak, so it won't be long before we start getting some useful information. Whoever this guy is, he must have been seen by someone."

"I hope so. This is going to make a lot of people very nervous. A break-in in broad daylight, and attempted arson on top of that. Maybe we should give a joint statement—before all kinds of wild stories start going around and people really start to panic."

"Good idea," he said. "Though I'd prefer to wait until we know some more."

"Deal," she said, patting him on the beefy arm. "I have to get back. I've got a land development application on my desk right now that needs looking at."

"A land development application? For…"

She grimaced. "A new shopping mall."

Alec's face fell. "A shopping mall—but Charlene!"

"I know what you're going to say, and I hear you, but we still have to do this by the book, and look at it from every angle. A new mall doesn't necessarily have to be a bad thing, you know." When he raised an eyebrow, she added, "Just trust me, all right?"

"All right," he said, but it was obvious he wasn't exactly bowled over by the idea of adding a shopping mall to the town landscape.

She waved to the rest of Alec's family, and then took her leave. She hadn't told her boyfriend, but the people pitching the plan for the new mall were actually coming in for a personal chat, and she couldn't afford to be late for the meeting.

§♣.

Alec watched his girlfriend carefully navigate the attic ladder, disappearing from view, and he must have been frowning, for when his sister wandered over, the first question she asked was, "And? Do you still have a girlfriend or did she dump you?"

He smiled. "She's sticking around… for now. Though the whole cat-talking thing really freaked her out."

"I'm sorry she had to find out like this," said Marge.

"It's fine. She had to find out sooner or later, and maybe better sooner than later."

"I hope you told her to keep this between ourselves?"

"Of course. Charlene isn't going to talk—you don't have to worry about that."

Marge glanced up at her big brother. "Something else bothering you? I mean, apart from the burglary, the attempted catslaughter and the fact that your girlfriend just discovered that your sister, niece and mother can talk to cats?"

"There's talk of a new shopping mall," he said. "She's looking at the application."

"But we already have a mall."

The next town over, Hampton Keys, had a great mall, which was only a twenty-minute drive away. It had been servicing the neighboring towns of Hampton Cove and Happy Bays for years, with no one asking for a second shopping center to be built.

"Yeah, I know."

"A mall is going to destroy Main Street."

"I know."

"It's going to attract a massive amount of traffic, all rolling through town."

"I know, I know."

"And tourists."

"Marge—"

"Tourists that are going to run roughshod over our peaceful little town."

"Look, I know all that, all right? But it's not my decision to make. Charlene is mayor, and it's her responsibility to weigh the pros and cons and make a measured decision."

"You can always give her a nudge in this or that direction, though, right?" asked Marge, giving her brother a nudge with her elbow.

"Oh, I'll nudge her plenty. Question is, is she going to listen?"

And that's what worried him: if she chose to go full steam ahead with this new mall development, and he was dead set against it, it might create a rift between them that could be hard to bridge. Plus, he didn't want to see their lovely little town fall into the hands of the kinds of developers who only had quick—and big—profits on their minds.

"I'm sure it'll all work out for the best," said Marge now, always the picture of optimism. "So what are we going to do about the cats? They need protecting, Alec. In case this person comes back."

"I'm not sure," he said, rubbing his face thoughtfully. "It's not as if I can ask a couple of uniforms to sit outside and guard the house twenty-four-seven."

"Why not?"

"Honey, if I tell my people to guard four cats they're going to think I'm crazy."

"Mh," said Marge. "Yeah, I can see how that would cause you all kinds of trouble." Then her face lit up. "I've got it. Why don't you ask Chase?"

"Chase?" he said with a twinge of alarm.

"Sure! He knows how much Max, Dooley, Harriet and Brutus mean to this family, right? And he's a cop. And he lives right next door. It's the perfect solution!"

"I don't know if…"

"Chase!" Marge bellowed. "Come here a second, will you?"

Chase dutifully came striding over. "What's up?" he asked.

"Tell him, Alec," said Marge, hooking her arm through her brother's.

"Tell me what?" asked Chase.

Alec cleared his throat. "The thing is, Chase, that this madman—well, it's not entirely inconceivable that he could come back."

"Uh-huh."

"And we don't want that, do we?"

"Oh, no, of course not."

"So we need someone to be stationed at the house... to watch... the cats."

"Great idea."

"So we were thinking about you, Chase," said Marge, patting the cop on the broad chest. "You wouldn't mind, would you?"

"Me?" asked Chase, darting an anxious look at his superior officer.

But Alec held up his hands. "Look, someone's gotta do it, buddy. And it might as well be you."

"But, Chief!"

"You don't want your girlfriend's cats to be harmed, do you?"

"No, but..."

"Well, then."

"But, Chief—what are the colleagues going to say?"

Chase's colleagues would have a field day laughing their asses off, thought Alec, but instead he said, "We'll simply tell them you're staking out the house in case this arsonist comes back. No mention of the cats will be made."

"But they'll know, Chief. I don't know how, but they'll know that you've turned me into a glorified catsitter!"

He was definitely right about that. "Nah, I'm sure they won't."

"Yeah, they will!" said Chase. "I'll be the joke of the force!"

"No, you won't."

"I think it's mighty nice of you to volunteer for this task,

Chase," said Marge. "And I'm sure Odelia will be overjoyed, too, knowing you're here to watch out for our babies."

With these words, Marge walked off to check out that dresser the burglar-slash-arsonist-slash-cat killer had been so interested in.

"Chief?" said Chase, his voice a little tremulous. "Please?"

"It's out of my hands, buddy," said Alec. "And for it's worth, I think you'll do great."

And then he walked off, too, leaving his deputy to stare after him looking crushed.

A man had to be made of stone not to feel sorry for the poor schmuck, but then sometimes you had to take one for the team, even though this particular team would probably start creating memes and post them on Facebook before the day was through.

5

I found Dooley in the kitchen, staring at my water bowl for some reason.

"Everything okay, Dooley?" I asked.

"Have you ever peed in someone else's water bowl, Max?" my friend asked, showing me that not everything was A-okay in the world of Dooley.

"Um, no, I don't think I have," I admitted.

"I'll bet plenty of cats have," he said. "And even though I confessed, I'm not sure many others would. And if that's true, how do we know that the water we drink is clean, Max?"

"I guess we never know for sure," I said, even though I could already see that my answer was potentially going to cause me no end of trouble.

"There's only one solution. I think we should ask Odelia to get rid of our bowls."

"I'm sure there are other solutions."

"Nope. Only one solution. No more water bowls."

"But Dooley, we have to drink. It's very important we stay hydrated, especially with all the dry food we eat."

"No, I know that, Max." He trounced up to one of Odelia's

high kitchen stools, and effortlessly jumped up. "Look at this," he said, and so I followed his example, though with slightly more effort required.

"What is it?" I asked once I'd arrived at my destination.

On the kitchen table was the tablet computer that Odelia got for us, in case we wanted to look up something on the internet. Dooley expertly flicked the thing to life, and I saw that he'd already looked up a page, for the browser depicted an intricate-looking device.

"This is a water dispenser," he said proudly. "It dispenses water."

"Oh-kay."

"There's a video." He started a video on the sales site, and it showed me exactly what a water dispenser does. Dooley was right: it dispensed water, which was to be expected.

"Pretty cool," I said, earning myself a proud smile from my friend.

"They have one for kibble, too. It dispenses kibble, not water."

"Okay," I said, seeing his point. "So let's ask Odelia to get us one of these, shall we? That way we can always be sure that the water we drink is fresh and not tampered with."

"Oh, Max, I'm so glad you agree. I thought you were going to give me all kinds of objections."

"Why would I give you all kinds of objections? This is the perfect solution for a household with four cats: instead of four bowls that Odelia constantly has to fill, she can now fill this baby up and there will always be plenty of water for all of us."

Dooley stared at me. "You mean you want her to buy one… for the four of us?"

"Of course."

"No, Max," he said, shaking his head. "She has to buy four

of these water dispensers. I can't possibly drink from your water dispenser, and you can't drink from mine."

I wanted to heave a deep sigh, but refrained from doing so. When Dooley has something on his mind, it's very hard to get him to let go of the idea.

"Fine. Let's run it by Odelia, and see what she says," I said, and made to jump down again.

"Wait, Max. There's something else I wanted to show you." And with a flick of the paw, he swiped to another page, this one depicting that famous TV show Paw Patrol. "Look, Max," he said. "It's a dog… that is also a cop!"

"It's a TV show for kids, Dooley," I pointed out. "In real life dogs can't be cops."

"No, but they can. Some dogs are trained as police dogs, you see. They go through this whole training program." And once again he was swiping away, and this time he landed on a website that showcased how some dogs are indeed trained as police dogs, and how they're very proficient at helping out their human colleagues. "See? They can sniff out drugs, and they can chase suspects… They're indi… spensable," he said, reading from one of the promo banners on the page.

I eyed the page for a moment, then shrugged. "So?"

"So maybe we should ask Odelia to hire one of these Paw Patrol dogs. So the dog can protect us in case the man who locked us in that chest comes back."

I frowned. "You want Odelia to hire a dog to protect her cats?"

"Exactly! These dogs catch bad men all the time, so why not our bad man?"

"Cause we're cats, Dooley. Cats take care of themselves. They don't need dogs."

"But—"

I held up my paw. "Cats don't need dogs to save them, Dooley. That's rule number one of being a cat."

"But we almost died up there, Max. So maybe we're not as good at taking care of ourselves as we think?"

I didn't know what to say to that. He had a point, of course, but hiring a dog to watch over us? That was simply too ludicrous to consider.

"Or we could always join this training program," he said, clicking on a video. "So we're ready when this person attacks us again."

We both watched as a few snippets from the dog training program were shown. It frankly made my stomach turn. Dogs were forced to jump through hoops—literally—and scale large obstacles, and even cross small streams. It all looked extremely exhausting.

"I don't think I want to do that, Dooley," I said when the video had run its course and so had the dogs. "I mean, I really, really don't want to do that."

"I think it would be good for you, Max."

"No, it won't."

"It will make you strong."

"I am strong already."

"It will make you fit."

"I'm perfectly fit."

"Then I suggest we hire a guard dog."

Faced with these two options, I have to admit neither one looked very appealing to me. I didn't want to be protected by a dog, and I didn't want to be trained as a member of Paw Patrol either. But on the other hand Dooley was right: we had to do something, for it had been proved beyond a reasonable doubt that we weren't ready in case of an attack.

"Fine," I said finally. "So maybe we should go ahead with your scheme."

He perked right up. "Do you really mean that, Max?"

"Yes, I do," I said, though not wholeheartedly, as you can imagine.

"Great!" he said. "I'll go and tell Odelia right away!"

And happy as a Paw Patrol puppy, he jumped down from the stool and pranced off.

Sometimes, I thought, Dooley's excitement was really tiring. Then again, maybe that just proved he was right: I was unfit, untrained, and as such the perfect target.

So… time to get some police cat training in?

Ugh.

6

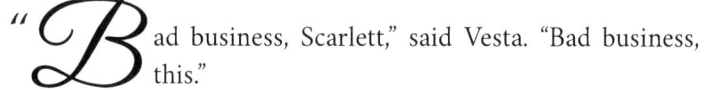

"Bad business, Scarlett," said Vesta. "Bad business, this."

"You can say that again," Vesta's friend Scarlett agreed.

The two women were seated in the outdoor dining area of the Hampton Cove Star, their small town's boutique hotel, and sipping from their respective favorite beverages: a hot chocolate with extra cream in Vesta's case, and a flat white for Scarlett. Both women might be the same age, but they couldn't have looked more different, and if an innocent bystander were asked to guess their ages, they'd have pegged Scarlett to be in her late fifties to early sixties, and Vesta in her late seventies to early eighties. Vesta, dressed in her usual tracksuit and sensible white shoes, had that whole Golden Girls look down pat, while Scarlett wouldn't have looked out of place in the best little whorehouse in Texas, with her thick russet curls, her inflated chest, and her face not revealing a single line.

"You simply don't expect this kind of violence in a small town like ours," Vesta continued. "Breaking and entering alone is a rare thing, and this attempted murder of four innocent pets? That's just wicked."

"Wicked," Scarlett agreed wholeheartedly. "Probably some uptown lowlife deciding to hit the suburbs for a change. But he'll soon discover we're not as soft on crime down here as he might have supposed."

"I don't know, Scarlett," said Vesta musingly. "I mean, you would expect my son to assemble his troops and hunt this animal down, but instead all he can think about is his girlfriend."

"Charlene Butterwick? Is that still a thing?"

"Oh, yes. Very much so, in fact."

"I would have thought that after finding out about your cat-talking trick she'd have run for the hills."

"No, she's a keeper, that one. Sticking it out. Which may or may not be a good thing."

"She's got your son distracted."

"Exactly. And a distracted chief of police is the last thing we need right now."

Scarlett shared a keen look with her friend. "I smell an opportunity for the watch, Vesta."

"I'm way ahead of you, darling. I've already told Father Reilly and Wilbur, and we're going on our first-ever patrol tonight."

"This night?"

"This night."

"Woo-hoo!"

"We're going to patrol this neighborhood to within an inch of its life. And I'd like to see this heartless animal try and strike again. He's going to have us to contend with."

"We're taking that sucker down!" Both women smiled before themselves, thinking pleasant thoughts about the neighborhood watch's watchful prowess, then Scarlett said,

"We're not going to patrol the neighborhood in that little red Peugeot of yours, are we?"

"I thought maybe we could ask Alec to borrow one of his squad cars. Seeing as he's not using them anyway."

"I like your thinking," said Scarlett, her eyes lighting up. "Ooh—and maybe we should get us some snazzy neighborhood watch outfits, too!"

"Again, way ahead of you." And Vesta reached into the shopping bag dangling from her chair and took out what at first glance looked like a beige jumpsuit.

"What is that?" asked Scarlett, giving the thing a look of abject disgust.

"The new neighborhood watch uniform," said Vesta proudly, and unfolded the thing to show it to Scarlett in all its splendor—or horror.

It *was* a jumpsuit, or at least that's what it looked like to Scarlett. "I'm not wearing that," she said decidedly after giving the monstrosity a glance. "Nuh-uh. No way."

"But why? It's got a logo and everything. See?" Vesta pointed to the little logo sewn onto the jumpsuit's chest. It depicted a stern-looking figure pointing at the innocent observer and saying, 'I've got my eye on you!' The figure looked a little too much like Vesta to be a coincidence, Scarlett thought. The whole thing was tacky to a degree.

"*You* can wear that thing, but I'm not wearing it," she repeated.

Vesta stared at her creation. "What's wrong with it?"

"What's wrong with it? We're going to look like a couple of morons, that's what. Have you even tried it on?"

"Sure. I tried it on this morning after the UPS man dropped it off. I ordered them online—I even designed the logo myself."

"Of course you did."

Vesta's look of confusion was replaced with one of censure. "What's that supposed to mean?"

"It's you!"

"No, it's not."

"It's clearly you, Vesta."

"Well, I had to use a model, and so I figured I might as well use myself. Here. Is that better?" And she ripped off the logo and handed the outfit to Scarlett, who immediately dumped it on the next chair, her face showing her extreme contempt for the thing. "I've got one for Wilbur, one for you, and one for Father Reilly, too," said Vesta, as she emptied the bag and placed them all on the table, next to the plate of pretty little pastries.

"No way in hell is Wilbur going to wear that thing—or Francis, for that matter."

"Of course they will. And look, I even got these for the cats, in case they want to ride along with us." And she held up four miniature beige outfits, perfect for cats.

Scarlett had to admit they were cute. "Look, I appreciate all the work you put into this, but I'm not wearing that —ever."

"But—"

"You can look like a ghostbuster if you want, Vesta. I prefer to look like Sigourney Weaver instead. How about that? Three ghostbusters and one hot crime-fighting mama."

"Ghostbuster?" asked Vesta, frowning. "What's a ghostbuster?"

"Wear that outfit and you'll know. Now let's talk guns. We can't go out there unarmed—especially if big-city crime has suddenly decided to sweep into town."

"I've got that covered," said Vesta, her smile returning, and she placed two futuristic-looking gadgets on the table, on top of the ghostbusters jumpsuits.

"What's that? asked Scarlett. "Water pistols?"

"Stun guns," said Vesta. "Perfectly legal, too, and they pack a lot of juice."

"Stun guns," said Scarlett doubtfully.

"Zap the bad guys with these things and they won't know what hit them."

"They'll know they haven't been hit with a real gun, that's for sure," said Scarlett, picking one up and turning it this way and that. Then she shrugged. "I guess it's better than nothing. What else have you got?"

"Pepper spray," said Vesta, "and this." And she placed something on the table that looked like a cane.

"What's this?" asked Scarlett. "Is your hip acting up again?"

"It's a club," said Vesta proudly.

"It's a cane."

"It's a club! The website said so."

"Oh, Vesta," murmured Scarlett. If she sounded disappointed, it was because she was. "I don't know about this," she said finally after swinging the club and almost hitting a passing waiter. "If we're going up against big-city crime, I just think we need big-city firepower."

"No can do, I'm afraid," said Vesta. "For one thing, I don't have a license, and neither do you, and for another, my son would never allow us to carry weapons in his town."

"Who cares what Alec thinks? We can't fight crime with our hands tied behind our backs, Vesta."

"Well, I do have Jack's shotgun," said Vesta, musingly. "I keep it in the garden shed."

"Now, *that's* what I'm talking about."

"Don't tell Alec, though, or he'll confiscate it."

"I don't get it. Since when are you so afraid of what your son thinks?"

Vesta sighed. "It's not just Alec. It's all of them." She ticked them off on her fingers: "Chase is a cop, Alec is a cop, Odelia is a private dick, and Charlene is the Mayor. And sometimes I've got the feeling they're all conspiring against me. It's tough being a weak old lady having to fight off an entire army of law enforcement."

Scarlett smirked. "Honey, you've faced off against bigger enemies. Remember how we used to tussle all the time?"

"Oh, do I?" said Vesta with a wistful gleam in her eye. "Those were the good old days."

"The Vesta I knew didn't take prisoners, and she never, ever backed down from a fight."

Vesta nodded, her shoulders sagging. "The Vesta you're talking about is long gone. I don't know what's going on, but when I woke up this morning I felt old. Old and tired."

"You probably forgot to take your vitamins."

"It's not that. It's having no allies in my own home. Always having to fight alone."

"What are you talking about? You've got me now, hun. And the rest of the watch. We're your allies."

Vesta perked up at that. "You mean that?"

"Sure I mean that. I'm in your corner now, Vesta. And I can assure you I've got plenty of fight left in me. Enough fight for the both of us."

Vesta smiled, and that holy fire was back, Scarlett saw to her satisfaction. "Thanks, Scarlett. I guess I needed to hear that."

"But being in your corner doesn't mean I'm wearing that ass-ugly outfit—no way."

Vesta laughed "Fine. You can wear whatever the hell you want. And tonight? We're going to kick some ass!"

7

Dooley glanced at his friend Max and wasn't happy with what he saw. Max looked preoccupied, he thought. Worried. And he was pretty sure it had something to do with this whole peeing-in-the-water-bowl episode.

Max was a kind cat—sometimes too kind for his own good. And Dooley was absolutely sure that Max had taken the incident very badly indeed, but was too nice to say it.

Dooley couldn't imagine what it would be like for your best friend to abuse your trust like that. To do something so heinous and so gross, and then to come right out and just… blurt it out like that.

It was something that had been preying on his mind for the past couple of days now, ever since it happened, and he'd been thinking about telling Max the whole time but had been afraid to. And then with the fire, and death suddenly staring them right in the face, he'd just blurted it out, and now he'd have to live with the consequences: Max's trust in him was obviously completely and utterly shattered, that was only to be expected, and it would take him a long time to learn how to trust again—if he ever would.

Dooley hopped down from his spot on the couch and walked over to the window again, to see if Odelia had arrived home yet. He wanted those water dispensers in place as soon as possible, to alleviate some of the damage he'd done.

He glanced over to Max again, and thought he caught his friend looking over to the kitchen, where his water bowl was placed, and Dooley knew exactly what he was thinking: if Dooley peed in my water bowl once, what's going to stop him from doing it again? And how will I know?

Oh, the shame! The shame!

Dooley heaved a long and tremulous sigh. Replacing that water bowl with a dispenser wasn't enough to make Max trust him again. Bigger and more drastic measures needed to be taken, and so he vowed to take them right this minute.

And then he was walking up to Max, and solemnly announced, "Max, I'm going to stop drinking."

"Mh?" said Max, looking up.

"I said I'm going to stop drinking from now on."

"And why would you do a silly thing like that?" asked Max, his glance frosty and his tone cold as ice. Clearly Max hated him right now. As well he should!

"Because when I don't drink, I won't have to pee, and when I don't have to pee, I won't accidentally pee in your bowl again."

"Oh, Dooley," said Max, annoyance making his eyes shoot javelins at his former friend.

"Just letting you know, Max," said Dooley, walking away again. "Just letting you know."

"Dooley!" said Max, but Dooley was already slouching off. He simply couldn't bear the look in his former friend's eyes: a look of sheer contempt and extreme loathing. And who could blame him? Not Dooley!

I stared after my friend, wondering what had gotten into him this time. Dooley sometimes has a habit of seeing trouble where there's no trouble at all, but stop drinking? That was extremely unhealthy, as far as I could tell. But since I was too busy trying to figure out why this assailant who'd attacked us in Marge and Tex's attic had done what he did, I soon found my mind returning to this most baffling question.

Odelia must have wondered the same thing, for when she breezed in through the sliding glass doors a few minutes later, the first thing she said was, "I don't get it, Max. Do you?"

"No, I don't get it either," I confessed.

"If he was a burglar, why didn't he take anything? And if he was a pet killer, why did he use such a roundabout way? Unless he simply panicked when he saw you guys?"

"Usually people panic when they see a dog," I pointed out. "Cats are not often considered a threat to your run-of-the-mill burglar."

Odelia had walked up to the fridge and took out a bottle of cold water and poured herself a glass. "My uncle assigned Chase guard duty tonight," she announced with a twinkle in her eye.

"Guard duty? Who is he guarding?"

"You guys!" said Odelia with a laugh. "And he's not happy about it."

"So… he's going to sit out there in his car and guard us?"

"I think he'd prefer to sit in here and guard you," said Odelia. "And since he can't be on guard twenty-four hours, Uncle Alec will have to find a second person."

"Dooley had a great idea," I began.

"Oh, I know. He told me all about it. I was skeptical at

first, but I'm starting to see his point. I'll have to talk to my uncle, but I think it can probably be arranged."

"Great," I said, though I wasn't really feeling all that great about the prospect of having to go into cat police academy training. Then again, sometimes the circumstances are such that you simply have no other option than to take the least desirable one.

"Dooley also said something about water and kibble dispensers?"

"Yeah, he feels bad about having done his business in my water bowl. And it got him thinking about who else might be doing the same thing."

"I'm sure you've got nothing to worry about, Max," said Odelia. "I change your water every day, so…"

"Oh, I know. And I'm sure that if someone did pee in my bowl, I'd smell it and tell you." And the fact that I hadn't, at any point in the last couple of weeks, smelled anything funny about my water, led me to think that Dooley might have made a mistake, and hadn't, in fact, peed in my water bowl, but one of the other bowls instead, possibly Harriet's, or Brutus's, and since they often drank next door, where we also had an array of bowls, they never even found out. And since Odelia changed the water every day, Dooley's little tinkle had simply been chucked down the sink, no harm done.

I'd meant to tell him, but I'd been so preoccupied with this whole burglary business that it had slipped my mind.

"So does your uncle think this man will be back?" I asked now.

"No idea. But if he does come back, he'll have Chase to contend with this time. And I can assure you that is a prospect any would-be burglar or pet killer would be wise to avoid."

8

Chase walked into the police station thinking hard thoughts about his superior officer throwing him under the bus like that. He was a detective, for crying out loud—not a glorified catsitter.

Dolores, the station dispatcher and receptionist, saw him come in and said, "Is it true what they're saying, Chase? That you're guarding your girlfriend's cats from now on?"

"Oh, don't you start, too," he grumbled as he joined Dolores for a chat. The red-haired middle-aged receptionist was a garrulous woman, and liked nothing better than to shoot the breeze with anyone who passed through her vestibule or happened to call in with some urgent or less urgent complaint.

"That's what you get from being henpecked, Detective," said Dolores in her trademark rasp. Then she gave him a wink. "Or I should probably say catpecked, huh?"

"Yeah, yeah," he muttered, idly leafing through her logbook. "Apparently the Chief thinks I'm the best man for the job, and who am I to question the big guy's judgment?"

"Oh, I think you're perfect for the job," said Dolores. "And

I'm sure with you around those cat killers won't stand a chance."

"It is a particularly heinous kind of crime," he mused. "I mean, who in their right mind would lock up a couple of innocent pets and set them on fire? You have to be a really evil person to do a thing like that." The whole episode had upset him to a degree. He hated violence against the innocent and the harmless, and pets were about the most innocent and harmless you could find. "When I get my hands on that piece of…"

"And I'm sure you will, Detective," said Dolores knowingly. "So what was that guy doing in Marge's attic is what I would like to know."

"No idea. Apparently looking at some old photo albums. Marge and Tex's wedding pictures. Though what anyone would want with those is frankly beyond me."

"A mystery most baffling," said Dolores. "So have you two set a date yet?"

"Oh, sure. September the fifth is the big day. Haven't you gotten your invitation yet?"

"No, sir, I have not." She shrugged. "I just figured you'd want to celebrate with friends and family only, and throw a separate party for colleagues at a later date or something."

"No, I want you there, Dolores. It wouldn't be the same without you."

"Gee, thanks," said Dolores, clearly tickled pink at these words.

"I'll ask Odelia. She's been handling that kind of stuff, together with her mom and grandma."

Dolores's smile disappeared. "Well, that explains it, then."

"What?"

"If Vesta is involved in the wedding preparations she'll probably have vetoed me. Me and her don't exactly get along."

"And why doesn't that surprise me?" said Chase with a smile. Vesta was an acquired taste, and more often than not rubbed people the wrong way.

"Is she still going ahead with this neighborhood watch thing of hers?"

"Yeah, that's still going strong."

"Bad idea, if you ask me. The Chief should never have allowed his mom to play amateur cop like that. She'll create more trouble than she's worth, her and Scarlett Canyon."

"I think it's all pretty harmless," he said, tapping the counter and turning to go. "And as long as she's out there patrolling the streets, she can't cause trouble someplace else."

"Hm," said Dolores doubtfully. "Leave it to Vesta to cause trouble all over the place. Mark my words, Chase. The Chief will rue the day he set that woman loose on these fine streets of ours."

And as Chase walked on, he wondered if Dolores was right. But then he figured the boss knew what he was doing. He had, after all, more experience dealing with his mother than anyone else in the precinct.

※

Charlene smiled at her guests. The two men could have been twins if she hadn't known better: both were wearing identical charcoal suits, their hair perfectly coiffed by what looked like the same hairdresser, and they were even wearing the same glasses. The only difference between Mark Dawson and James Blatch, as far as she could determine, was that one was in charge of the proceedings, and the other was merely along for the ride.

"So you see, Madam Mayor," said Mr. Blatch as he indicated the tablet on her desk. "Construction on the mall will provide plenty of jobs, and once the mall is operational, that will increase even more. Of course we'd prefer to recruit our workforce locally."

"You did your homework, Mr. Blatch," she said, leaning back. "But what you haven't taken into consideration is the economic impact on the heart of our town. With so many new stores opening, don't you think the town center will lose its appeal?"

"I can assure you that this whole 'death of Main Street' is simply a myth, Madam Mayor," said the extremely tanned businessman with an indulgent smile. "The truth is that more shops means more shoppers, and those shoppers will also want to visit Main Street, and spend their hard-earned money on the local stores. Your town will thrive!"

"I'm not so sure about that," said Charlene. "Do you have hard evidence that this is the case? Projections, studies, things like that?"

"Oh, absolutely. And I'll be more than happy to share them with you."

The guy was a smooth talker, but then that was probably a given, as he was trying to sell her on an entire mall. She glanced up when the phone on her desk started ringing. She pressed a button. "I thought I said I didn't want to be disturbed, Imelda," she began.

"It's Chief Alec, Ma'am," said her secretary, her voice betraying her distress. "He says it's urgent."

Her heart skipped a beat as she picked up the phone and threw her guests a reassuring glance and held up her finger. "Chief?" she said, listening intently.

"Charlene—it's your uncle. He's been in an accident."

"My uncle? How…"

"Charlene, honey." The Chief's voice turned sorrowful. "I'm afraid he didn't make it."

9

Tex wasn't in a particularly good mood. When a man's house is being burgled, and his cats are being attacked in his very own home, it's enough to put any person off his game, and it was with this recent tragedy in mind that he now invited his next patient into his office. Usually this was Vesta's job, but as usual his mother-in-law had decided to renege on her duties and instead gallivant all over town and play amateur cop instead.

It was one more thing to set the seal on his gloom, and as he tried to spirit a welcoming smile on his face so as not to scare off this new patient of his, he mentally wished for this long day to end already so he could go home and ascertain whether the security company his daughter's future husband had promised he'd get in touch with, had secured his home to such an extent that it was now burglar-proof.

"Take a seat, please, Mr…" he said. It rarely happened that he saw a new patient these days, most of his patients were regulars who'd found their way to his office years ago.

The young man didn't speak, and accepted his invitation to take a seat in silence. He was a clean-cut young man, and wouldn't have looked out of place in a recruitment video for Mormon elders. His white shirt was crisp, his slacks perfectly creased, and he was wearing a nice paisley tie. Even his hair looked cut from the same mold Barbie's Ken was cut from. The only thing that detracted from the picture of what could have been absolute male perfection were his ears, which stood out from his head a little.

"So what can I do for you?" asked Tex as he took a seat behind his desk and rested his elbows on his blotter, his fingers interlaced, projecting the image of the capable doctor.

"This may surprise you, Dr. Poole," said the young man, "but I'm actually not here as a patient."

"Oh?" said Tex. But then he got it. He pointed at the man. "I know who you are."

"You do?"

"Sure. Sales rep for a pharmaceutical company. Am I right or am I right?" And he smiled the kind of smile that said, 'Give me your best shot, salesman person, and please make sure to add the words Ten-day Cruise and Five-star Hotel to your sales pitch.'

But much to his surprise the young man shook his head. "I'm actually here for personal reasons," he said, causing Tex to frown.

"Personal reasons?"

"Yes. You are Doctor Tex Poole, right?"

"That's me."

The young man smiled an engaging smile, and it was as if the sun suddenly broke through the cloud deck. He thrust out a hand. "My name is Dudley Checkers, Dr. Poole. But you probably know me as Jaqlyn's son."

"I do?"

"My mom told me all about you."

"Jaqlyn... Checkers you say?" Tex threw his mind back...

and a vague recollection stirred of a mousy brown-haired girl with freckles, braces and a lisp.

"She told me how you met, and how you were the love of her life."

Tex gulped a little at this. "Love of her life, eh?"

"Sure. Don't you remember? The only reason she broke up with you is because her parents made her. They were Western Baptists, and didn't take kindly to their daughter dating a person who wasn't a member of their church. It broke her heart, Dr. Poole."

"Is that so?" he said, still trying to remember who this Jaqlyn person was exactly.

"And then when she discovered she was pregnant, of course there was hell to pay."

"Pregnant!" he said. The plot was thickening—in fact it was thickening so fast Tex's head was spinning.

"Her folks wanted her to have the baby, of course, and I can tell you, Dr. Poole, that I never stinted for love and affection. Oh, no, sir, I did not." The young man's smile turned positively Hollywoodian now—wide and toothy. "Mom told me the whole story last month. She died, you see, and didn't want to leave this world without laying it all out for me—a tearful moment, I can tell you. She told me to go and meet my dad… and gave me his name." The kid then stuck out his hand. "I'm so happy to finally meet you… Daddy!"

੩

"How did it happen?" asked Charlene as she stared down into the empty pool.

"He must have lost his balance," said Alec. "If it's any consolation, he never knew what happened. Simply fell in and… well, died."

She nodded. She'd always been fond of this uncle of hers,

even though they hadn't been in touch all that much lately. Since becoming mayor of Hampton Cove her schedule had been pretty crammed, and then with romance suddenly sweeping into her life…

She placed a hand on her boyfriend's arm, and he hugged her close. "We're still asking around, but so far the story checks out: he was out here, inspecting the work when it happened. No one else around."

"He'd always been fond of his job. Said building pools was the best job in the world. And he was good at it, too. Best pool builder in the county."

"I know. If I was in the market for a pool I'd have hired your uncle. He was the best."

They were in the backyard of a villa that was still under construction. The owners had decided to go all in and had hired Frank Butterwick to put in a pool.

"If only he'd fallen in at the shallow end," said Charlene as she wiped away a tear.

Abe Cornwall, the county coroner, looked up from his inspection of the body. "Not much I can tell you that you don't already know," he said, addressing the Chief. "Contusions consistent with a fall from this height. Death was instantaneous, I'd say."

"Thanks, Abe," said Alec, and gently led Charlene away from the grisly scene. "I've already called your mom and dad. They'll be here soon."

She glanced up when she saw a couple of her uncle's workers, talking animatedly amongst each other. "Did you talk to them?" she asked. "What did they say?"

"They weren't here when it happened. None of them were. Your uncle had a habit of being the first to arrive in the morning, and work out the day's schedule."

"Who found him?"

"That fellow over there," said Alec, pointing to a gangly

guy with an overbite. "Name is Grant Folkman. Do you want to talk to him?"

"Yeah, I'd like to," she said, so they walked over to where her uncle's men were standing around, and Alec nodded a greeting.

"This is Frank's niece," he introduced Charlene. "And this here is Grant. You found Charlene's uncle, isn't that right, Grant?"

"Yeah—big shock it was, too," said Grant, dropping down the stub of his cigarette and crushing it under his heel. "He was a great guy, Mrs. Butterwick."

"Miss," said Charlene, more out of habit than anything else. "How long have you worked for my uncle, Grant?"

"Oh, about three years now, I think? There wasn't a lot of turnover, which probably says something about Frank. He wasn't just a great guy, but a great boss, too."

"He could yell up a storm, though, couldn't he?" said one of Grant's colleagues.

"Yeah, Frank was definitely a yeller," said Grant with a smile. "But you knew he didn't mean it. He yelled but not in a nasty way, if you know what I mean."

She smiled. "Yeah, I think I do."

Grant gave her a shifty-eyed glance. "Do you—do you know what's going to happen now, Miss? I mean, with Frank gone and all?"

"No, I'm sorry but I wasn't involved in my uncle's business. Didn't he have a business partner?"

"Yeah, but he kinda disappeared," said Grant with a shrug.

"Disappeared? What do you mean?"

"Just that. He was here one day and gone the next. Frank wasn't happy about it, but what could he do?"

"And who was this business partner?" asked Alec.

"Um… well, personally I never met him, but I think his

name was Pollard? He was what you might call a silent partner?"

"Oh, he sure was silent, all right," said the other worker. "So silent we never saw him."

Charlene nodded. "I'm sure my family will sort it all out. My parents will be here soon, and my dad—he helped set up my uncle's business. I'm sure he knows all about it."

"Thanks, Miss Butterwick," said the young man with a nod.

And as Charlene and Alec walked off, she heard him say to his buddy, "Good-looking woman, that Miss Butterwick," and she smiled.

"I'll try to get in touch with this business partner," said Alec.

"No, don't bother. My dad will sort it all out. He's in charge now. He'll decide what to do with the business."

"Fair enough," said Alec, and gave her a look of concern. "Will you be all right?"

"Yeah, don't worry about me," she said with a wave of the hand. "I'll be just fine. I'll wait until my parents are here and then I have to get back."

"The mall meeting?"

"I canceled it. For now."

"Good," he said, making perfectly clear what he thought of the project.

10

I was sipping from my bowl of water when I noticed Dooley intently looking at me from the sidelines. It was a little disconcerting, to be honest. I'm one of those cats that don't like it when people look at them when they're eating or drinking. I don't know why, but it simply makes me nervous. Even when it's a close friend like Dooley doing the staring, it makes me a little giggly. And it made me more than a little giggly now.

"What?" I asked finally, when he wouldn't stop looking.

"How can you do that, Max?" he asked, shaking his head.

"Do what?" I asked as I licked the few drops of water dangling from my mustache.

"Drink without making sure if the water is clean."

I frowned at him. "I'm pretty sure that Odelia wouldn't give us bad water to drink," I said. "And besides, I also like to think that my sense of smell and my sense of taste are capable enough to make sure that this water is fine for feline consumption."

"But how can you be sure, Max?" he insisted. "How can you be absolutely sure?"

"Um... Well, I guess one can never be one hundred percent sure, but that's where trust features into the thing. I trust Odelia not to poison me, so there's that."

He shook his head sadly, then said, "Are you absolutely sure the water was fine?"

I glanced at my bowl, then back at my friend. "What do you mean?"

He suddenly gestured to a carton of grapefruit juice lying next to him. I recognized it as belonging to Chase, who likes all forms of fruit juice, and likes to switch things up, too.

"Are you sure the water didn't taste like... grape?" asked Dooley with a meaningful look in his eyes.

"I..." Giving the water another lick, I determined that yes, it did indeed taste a little bit like grapefruit juice. But just a hint, you know. I smiled at my friend. "You tricked me!"

"I did," he said gravely. "Just to show you that you can never be too careful."

And then understanding dawned. "Is this still about the peeing in my bowl thing?"

"Oh, Max! You say you would have noticed if I peed in your bowl. That Odelia must have changed the water before you had a chance to drink from that contaminated bowl. But I think what happened is you simply didn't pay attention and you drank that entire bowl. Just like you did now." His voice broke, and that mournful expression was back.

"Look, even if I did, no harm done, right? A little bit of pee won't kill me."

He gave me a look of profound shock. "Max, how can you say that! I tried to poison you and you're treating the whole thing so—so flippantly!"

"Because it's not a big deal," I said, and patted my friend on the back. "Hey, now. Don't feel bad, Dooley. We all make mistakes, and that's fine. No harm done, right?"

"Oh, Max," he said. "I don't deserve a friend like you. I

really don't." And with these words, he shuffled off, looking even more dejected than before.

And I would have gone after him to get it through that thick skull of his that it really wasn't a big deal, but then Gran waltzed in and made a beeline for me. "Max! Great news, buddy. The watch will be patrolling the streets of this neighborhood tonight, and if we see any sign of this cat killer, we'll nab him and nab him good!"

"Great," I said without much excitement.

"Aren't you thrilled?" she asked censoriously. "You should be thrilled. The watch is here to protect you. You and every other member of our neighborhood."

"No, it's just that… Dooley is acting really weird, and I don't know how to get him out of his funk."

"The watch can't help you there… but I can," she finished on a triumphant note. "I'll talk to that young whippersnapper, shall I? What seems to be the problem this time?"

"He peed in my water bowl and now he blames himself and figures I'm angry with him—which I'm not."

"Peed in your water bowl," said Gran, committing this to memory as she tapped her temple. "Got it. I'll get on it right away. Anything else?"

"No, that's it."

She picked me up and gave me a closer scrutiny. "No lingering effects from the fire?"

"No, I'm good."

"Are you sure? Cause I can get you a pet shrink if you want. Or a trauma specialist."

"No need," I said. "And with you patrolling the streets I feel so much safer already."

Her smile was infectious, and touching. "That's what I'm doing this for, Max. For people like you." And with these words, she put me down again and was off with a spring in her step. "The watch is watching!" she announced as she passed through the door and out into the backyard. "So watch out!"

I couldn't help but grin at this. And if she could make Dooley see the light, so much the better. And it was with a heart filled with hope that I set paw for the great outdoors myself. The sun was out in full force, and frankly I could do with a bit of fresh air. And I was just passing through the hole in the hedge and going in search of Brutus and Harriet when suddenly Tex came walking out of the house, a cleancut young man in tow.

Marge, who'd been hanging up the laundry, looked up.

"Marge, honey," said Tex. "I want you to meet someone. Dudley, this is Marge, my wife. Marge, this is Dudley Checkers. Dudley is… my son."

11

"He doesn't look like Tex," said Brutus.

"It's the ears," said Harriet. "Try to picture him without those floppy ears and I think he looks just like Tex."

"I think he looks like Marge," said Dooley.

"He can't look like Marge, Dooley," I said. "Marge isn't his mother."

The four of us were on the porch swing, intently watching the scene as it played out in the backyard. Tex had introduced his new son to his wife, and Marge was so taken aback she'd almost fallen on her tushy.

"I don't understand," said Dooley. "If Tex is Dudley's father, then Marge must be his mother, right?"

"Not necessarily," I said. "As I understand it Tex had a girlfriend before he met Marge and he and this girlfriend had, um, relations, and that's where this kid comes from."

Dooley chewed on that for a long moment. Judging from the thought wrinkle that appeared on his furry brow, it was tough going for a while, but finally he said, "So if he's Tex's son but not Marge's… what does that make him?"

"It makes him Marge's… stepson, I guess?" said Harriet. "And Odelia's stepbrother."

Dooley's eyes went a little wider. "Odelia has a brother?"

"Yeah, this guy we're looking at right now," said Brutus.

"But… he doesn't look like Odelia at all, so how can he be her brother?"

"Oh, Dooley," said Harriet with an eyeroll.

"What's going on?" asked Gran, who'd come out of the house munching on a cream cheese bagel and now took a seat next to us on the swing, her short legs dangling.

"Tex just found out he has a son," I said. "And he told Marge but I don't think she's happy about it."

Gran almost dropped her bagel. "Tex? A son? What the hell are you talking about?"

"This kid just introduced himself and said he's Tex's son," said Harriet with a shrug. "That's all I know."

"That's all any of us know," I said, with just a touch of chagrin. Usually we're the best-informed cats in Hampton Cove and now it appeared as if there was a very big secret that we hadn't been clued into, and it had hit very close to home, too.

"I don't believe this," said Gran, gawking at this Dudley character, who now stood beaming at Marge. "Tex has a son." She narrowed her eyes at the kid. "How old is he?"

"Um… probably in his late twenties?" I guessed.

"Huh," said Gran, and started munching her bagel again, though judging from the mechanical movements of her jaw she was thinking hard—almost as hard as Dooley.

"I don't know if I like this, Max," Dooley confessed. "A brother for Odelia. What does it mean?"

"What do you mean what does it mean? It means what it means," I said, becoming philosophical for a change.

"I mean is he going to move in with us? Or move in with Marge and Tex?"

"I doubt that very much," I said. "He probably has a place of his own. So why would he move in with us?"

"Great news, you guys!" Tex suddenly announced, including us in the conversation. "Dudley is moving in with us!"

"Oh, for God's sakes," said Gran, not sounding all that excited at the prospect of welcoming this new grandson of hers into the family.

"Tex!" said Marge suddenly. "Can I have a word? In private?" she added pointedly.

"Oh, sure. Make yourself at home, Dudley. *Mi casa es su casa* and all that, right?"

"Thanks, Dad," said Dudley. He looked as fresh-faced and excited to meet his dad as any son who's just met his long-lost dad for the first time.

Marge and Tex charged into the house and Marge slammed the kitchen door for good measure.

"Uh-oh," said Gran. "Looks like trouble in the family."

"Do you think Marge is unhappy about having a son?" asked Dooley.

"You can bet she is," said Gran, then muttered, "I'm going to have to shut up now, you guys. He's coming over to talk to me." And then she plastered the fakest smile on her face I'd ever seen outside of a soap opera finale, and said, "So nice to meet you… Dudley, is it?"

"Yes, ma'am," said Dudley, and held out a hand, which Gran shook after a moment's hesitation. And since her hand was smeared with cream cheese, Dudley's hand was now also smeared with cream cheese, which he didn't seem all that happy about.

"See, Max?" said Dooley. "That's how easy contamination can happen. And before you know it you're eating or drinking someone else's contaminants."

"Has Gran talked to you yet?" I asked.

"No, why?" he said. Then, alarmed, added, "She's not sick or dying, is she?"

"Gran is fine. It's you that's not fine. Harping on this pee incident the whole time."

"But it's important, Max!"

"Oh, will you please give it a rest already," said Harriet. "What's done is done, Dooley, so drop the subject, will you?"

"But—"

"It's happened to me many, many times, Dooley," said Brutus, placing a brotherly paw on my friend's shoulder. "And do you see me fretting? Do you see me making a big fuss?"

"It happened to you many times?" said Harriet with a laugh. "What do you mean?"

"Well, sometimes I have to pee so bad that I don't reach my litter box in time, and since I don't want to pee on the floor, or, God forbid, in a flowerpot, I often pick the first suitable receptacle I see, and in many cases that's one of the water bowls."

We all stared at the cat now. "What water bowls?" asked Harriet.

"Well, I try to be fair and square about it, so if I pick Max's bowl one day, I always try to pick Dooley's the next, or… yours…"

Harriet's eyes were shooting sheets of flame in the direction of her one and true love. "You mean to tell me that you've been peeing in my water bowl all this time?"

He gave her a guarded look. "Well, not *all* the time, if you see what I mean—just *some* of the time."

"Why don't you pee in your own bowl, Brutus?" I asked. "Why pee in ours?"

He stared at me thoughtfully. "Huh. I guess the thought has never occurred to me to pee in my own bowl. Though now that you mention it, maybe that's what I should have done from the beginning," he added when he caught Harriet's furious look amidships and rocked back a little.

"I can't believe you've been peeing in our bowls!" Harriet cried.

"Just a tinkle," he said. "The pre-pee, if you catch my drift. To tide me over until I can reach my litter box without having an accident. Just those first few drops, you know."

"Oh, I do know, and now I understand why my water sometimes tastes a little off."

"See, Max?" said Dooley. "You've been drinking Brutus's pee all this time and you didn't even notice."

"Well, so have you, Dooley," I pointed out, and watched my friend's face fall.

"Ewww!" he said. "I'm never drinking from my bowl again!"

Suddenly those water dispensers sounded like a great idea.

At least Brutus wouldn't be able to take a tinkle in those. Or would he?

12

Odelia was hard at work on her article about the attack on her cats that morning when her uncle waltzed into her office. She was surprised to see him, for he was usually not in the habit of visiting her at the Gazette offices.

"Hey, Uncle Alec," she said. And when she noticed the careworn expression on her uncle's face when he took a seat, she immediately feared the worst. "Did Charlene break up with you again?"

Immediately he gave her a look of indignation. "No, she did not. What makes you think that?"

"Oh, nothing," she said. "Just… you have that look."

"Charlene did not break up with me," he said emphatically. "Whatever people say." He eyed her intently. "Have people been saying that about us? Is that it?"

"No, I haven't picked up any gossip about you and Charlene lately."

Often people in Hampton Cove, when they had nothing better to do, enjoyed spending their time gossiping about anyone and everyone, and even when they didn't have time they still considered it their most beloved pastime for some reason.

"Charlene's uncle died this morning," he said, glancing around her office for a moment before settling his gaze on her again. "Looks like an accident. He installed pools for a living," he explained, "and he fell in at the deep end of an empty pool. Died on impact, according to Abe."

"That's terrible," said Odelia. "Was Charlene close with her uncle?"

"Not particularly, but she was fond of him. Well, you know how it is. You're close to all of your relatives when you're little, then you go off to college and start your career and those once close family bonds tend to fall by the wayside as you build your own life."

"Except for us," she said with a smile.

Her uncle reciprocated with a goofy smile of his own. "Yeah, except for our family. But anyway, I was thinking that if you don't have too much work on your hands right now that maybe you could look into this guy's death for me?"

She arched an inquisitive eyebrow. "You mean his *accident?*"

"Yeah, I'm not so sure about that."

"You think he was murdered?"

He shrugged his broad shoulders. "Honestly? No idea. Call it a hunch, but I have the feeling there's more to this than meets the eye."

"Sure, I'll look into it if you want. But is there a particular reason you're asking me and not one of your officers?"

"If the police get involved it will be in the context of an official police inquiry, and that's exactly what I don't want. I want everyone to think it's a simple accident."

"You don't want to alarm the murderer."

"*If* there is a murderer," he said.

"Gotcha."

"Oh, and I'd appreciate it if you didn't tell Charlene."

"You don't want her to know her uncle may have been murdered?"

"No, I don't. She's got enough on her plate as it is. And if I'm wrong about this, I don't want her to get all worked up about it for no reason."

"Sure. I'll be super-discreet." When her uncle didn't make any indication of getting up, she frowned. "Is there more?"

He scratched his nose. "Well, um… your grandmother just sent me a text. Looks like there's going to be a family extension."

"A family extension? What do you mean?"

"Yeah, a kid just came forward claiming he's your dad's son."

Odelia blinked. Whatever she'd been expecting, it most definitely wasn't this. "My dad's son? You mean…"

"Looks like your dad dated the kid's mom at some point and she ended up pregnant and had his baby." He held up his hands. "That's all I know."

"My dad… has a son," she said, highly taken aback by this unexpected piece of news. "I wonder how Mom is taking this."

"Knowing my sister, not well," said her uncle, who was still making no indication of having said his bit. "And in other news, your grandmother is going to start patrolling the streets at night, looking for that so-called cat killer."

"That's great," said Odelia, nodding. "I hope she catches the guy."

"Yeah, well, all I know is that when Vesta is out and about, trouble usually follows her around like a newborn pup." He got up. "Oh, and that dog you were asking about? I think I found just the one."

"You did? Hey, that's great!"

"Yeah, he's a bit long in the tooth maybe, but by all

accounts he used to be a fine police dog when he was still on active duty."

Her face fell. "You're getting me a retired dog?"

"Of course. What did you expect? That you were getting an active dog? Those are all spoken for, honey. But Rambo is a mighty fine specimen, so your cats will be absolutely safe." Her uncle flashed her a quick grin. "And he's had all his shots, too."

And with these words, he left the office, giving the doorframe a rap as he went.

A retired police dog to guard her cats, Grandma Muffin patrolling the streets and, most importantly, a stepbrother. No wonder her uncle felt the need to drop by in person.

She picked up her phone and called her mom but the call went straight to voicemail. So instead she called her grandmother, who picked up at the first ring.

"What do you want?" growled the older lady.

"Is it true that I have a stepbrother?" she asked.

Gran chuckled loudly. "Yeah, you do. And he's something else, too."

"That bad, huh?"

"No, that good. The perfect son! Very polite, very nice, and not too bad-looking either. Though he should probably do something about his ears, and that's exactly what I told him."

"His ears?"

"Yeah, you'll see. When are you coming home to meet your new brother?"

Her heart sank. "How is Mom taking it?"

"What do you think?"

"I'm guessing… not good?"

"You're guessing right. If I were in your father's shoes right now I'd want to be zapped up by Captain Kirk and taken aboard the Starship Enterprise to the far side of the galaxy."

"That bad, huh."

"Better get over here before she commits involuntary manslaughter is all I'm saying."

And as she disconnected, Odelia wondered where this new brother of hers had suddenly sprung from. Mom's worst nightmare, probably.

13

When Charlene returned to her office she was surprised that the two businessmen trying to sell her on the idea of a new shopping mall for Hampton Cove were still there.

She'd thought for sure they would have left by now.

Imelda, her secretary, made her aware of their presence when she said, in an exaggerated whisper, "They refused to leave! Said they preferred to await your return rather than reschedule!"

If she hadn't been in the mood to discuss the development of a shopping mall project before, she certainly wasn't now, after learning about the tragic death of her uncle. But she'd long ago accepted that a public servant wasn't always in control of their agenda, and that compromises would have to be made along the way.

So she waltzed into her office to find the same two gentlemen still seated at her desk, as if they hadn't moved a muscle. The only difference was that they'd brought out their model, and had placed it right on top of her desk.

She stared at the thing now, and had to admit that it looked pretty neat indeed.

"Ah, Madam Mayor," said Mr. Blatch, still rocking that incredible tan of his, and those shiny white teeth. "We were hoping you'd come back."

"Yeah, sorry about that," she said. "A family emergency."

"We absolutely understand," said Mr. Dawson, who was the more soft-spoken and reticent of the twosome. "I hope the news wasn't too bad?"

"My uncle died," she blurted out. "Fell into an empty pool and cracked his skull."

"Oh, I'm so sorry," said Mr. Blatch, his smile faltering.

"Terrible tragedy, I'm sure," said his colleague, closing his eyes and shaking his head.

There was a moment's silence after that—a respectable silence, Charlene liked to think, but the moment she opened her mouth to speak, both men's smiles returned and they proudly pointed to the model. "This is what she will look like," said Mr. Blatch.

"A gem, don't you think?" said Mr. Dawson.

"A jewel in Hampton Cove's crown."

"It looks pretty… impressive," she had to admit. And then she noticed the name written above the mall entrance: The Butterwick Mall.

"Do you like the name? We can always change it," said Mr. Dawson.

"How about the Charlene Shopping Center?" said Mr. Blatch.

"Or the Butterwick Galleria."

"Has a nice ring to it, wouldn't you agree, Madam Mayor?"

She smiled. She'd been in politics long enough to know when she was being played. "Look, I don't care about the name. I just want what's best for this town," she said.

"Oh, we absolutely agree," said Mr. Blatch.

"Absolutely," said Mr. Dawson. "Which is why we've gone to the trouble of acquiring the land the mall will be built on—just in case."

"Just in case," mimicked his fellow real estate developer.

"You already bought up all the land?" she asked.

"All except one plot," said Mr. Blatch.

"One teensy tiny plot of land."

"Unfortunately it's also the most important plot, as it's located right… there," said Mr. Blatch, and pointed to the center of the mall, where a very nice fountain stood.

"And who owns that land?" she asked, curious in spite of herself.

Mr. Blatch ceremoniously got out his phone and tapped it, then announced, "One Tex Poole, who acquired the land back in 1995 but then never developed it."

"It just sits there," said his colleague, shaking his head and tut-tutting slightly.

"Isn't that just sad? To buy a piece of land, ripe for building, and then never build?"

"Did you just say… Tex Poole?" asked Charlene, taken aback.

Both men nodded. "Yep. Tex Poole," said Mr. Blatch. "I have it right here on my phone so it must be right."

"We contacted Mr. Poole, and so far he's refusing to sell, unfortunately."

"Which is why we were hoping for the council's approval, so we can fast-track the process of buying him out."

"Or finding some other solution," said Mr. Dawson, giving her a knowing wink.

"Oh, no, you don't," she said.

Both men looked taken aback. "Oh, no, we don't what?" asked Mr. Blatch.

"You do know that Tex Poole is my boyfriend's brother-in-law, of course."

"Your brother-in-law?" asked Mr. Dawson, looking genuinely surprised.

"I can assure you that we didn't know, Madam Mayor," said Mr. Blatch.

"Absolutely no idea."

"None whatsoever."

They looked earnest enough, but then you never knew with these business types, Charlene thought. They could simply be using her to get to Tex, if he really did own that piece of land, and was refusing to sell.

"Look, we'll leave this here with you, how about that?" said Mr. Blatch, lovingly placing both hands on the model and giving it a gentle tap.

"And we'll let you discuss it with the members of the town council," said Mr. Dawson.

"And when you've made up your mind, please let us know at your earliest convenience."

"Because if we're going to pursue this, we need to move fast."

"Other towns are clamoring for this highly unique and promising project, and so we're not going to be able to leave this on the table for much longer."

"Another… five days, perhaps?"

"Let's make it seven," said his partner.

And then both men got up swiftly and held out their hands. She shook them and watched them leave, then returned her gaze to the model right under her nose.

It did look pretty darn impressive. A mall for Hampton Cove, and a mall carrying her name at that. Mom and Dad would be really proud if she would be able to pull this off.

But then she shook herself. She wasn't going to be

tempted by vanity. She needed to figure out if this was a good thing for the town or not, and not be swayed by ulterior motives.

Then again. The Butterwick Mall? It sounded pretty cool.

14

*D*inner was a family affair, as everyone wanted to meet Tex's new son in person. Even Uncle Alec and Charlene were there, and so was Scarlett, who's Gran's best friend.

We were all seated in Tex and Marge's backyard, though if the guests had expected Marge to lay out a nice big spread they were sadly mistaken. In fact Tex had had to order pizza because his wife made it clear that she would never, under any circumstances, cook for this son of his he hadn't told her about in the twenty-five years they'd been married.

I think it was safe to say that Marge was livid, and Tex looked distinctly ill at ease.

"So how did you find out that Tex was your dad?" asked Scarlett, who's never shy to ask the really tough questions. She would have made a great reporter, I reckoned.

"My mama told me before she died," said the kid, whose ears really were quite large.

"On her death bed, huh? How romantic," said Scarlett, with a distinct lack of tact.

"Yeah, she would have told me sooner but she was always

afraid to," said Dudley. "But when she got the diagnosis she knew she had to make a choice: take her secret into the grave, or tell me. And I'm glad she opted for the latter," he added, directing a proud glance at his father. "In fact I'm happy things turned out the way they did. Not with my mother dying, I mean, but with me finally finding my dad. Can you pass me the ketchup, Daddy?"

"Sure… son," said Tex awkwardly.

"So is it true that Dad offered for you to stay here?" asked Odelia now.

"Yeah, I'm in between homes right now? I was living with my mom the last couple of months, taking care of her. But since she died her sister, my Auntie Ellen, put the house on the market, and so I don't have anywhere to stay right now."

"You can stay in the attic," said Marge, earning herself a startled look from her husband.

"Honey, I thought he could take the spare bedroom."

"In case you've forgotten, we don't have a spare bedroom anymore, Tex," said Marge icily. "We turned it into a storage space," she explained for the sake of Dudley.

"Oh, but the attic is perfectly fine," said Dudley, squirting a big helping of ketchup on his pizza and then taking a big bite. "In fact any room will do. I'm used to living rough."

"Didn't your mother ever marry?" asked Gran, who is just as curious as Scarlett and just as shameless in her questions.

Dudley's face darkened. "I did have a stepdad for a while, but he wasn't the kindest man in the world." He shrugged. "What can I say? In between the beatings and the verbal abuse he was okay, I guess. But I was still happy when Mom finally kicked him out."

"That sounds pretty terrible," said Odelia with feeling.

"Yeah, it wasn't the best time of my life." The kid's face creased into a big smile. "But things are finally looking up now that I finally found my daddy."

"Yeah, I'll bet," said Gran, giving her daughter a curious look, which Marge pointedly chose to ignore.

"What do you think about Tex's new son, Max?" asked Dooley.

The four of us were lying a little ways away on the cooling lawn, observing the humans' interactions with a distinct sense of astonishment. It's not every day that suddenly your humans' number is expanded with the arrival on the scene of a new son.

"I'm not sure," I said. "He sure seems nice enough. But I don't like that he's causing this rift between Marge and Tex."

"He's causing a rift?!" asked Dooley, giving me a look of surprise.

"Oh, Dooley, can't you see yourself how hard Marge is taking this whole situation?" said Harriet. "She's obviously suffering."

Dooley studied Marge for a moment, then shook his head. "She looks all right to me."

"That's because you're a guy," said Harriet. "Guys always have a hard time putting themselves in the shoes of a girl."

"Why would I want to wear Marge's shoes?" asked Dooley. "I never wear shoes."

"Oh, Dooley," said Harriet with a sigh.

"I like him," said Brutus. "I think he looks just like Odelia. And if he would do something about those ears of his, I think I would probably like him even more."

"Which just goes to show what a superficial cat you really are," snapped Harriet. She'd obviously not forgiven her boyfriend for peeing in our bowls yet. "I just hope for your sake, *Brutus*, that you haven't been doing number two in our kibble bowls," she added, causing both Dooley and I to give her a look of horror.

"Number two in our kibble bowls!" Dooley cried.

"For the record," said Brutus stoically, "I did not—I repeat, I did not—do number two in your kibble bowls."

"Oh? And why would I believe you?"

"Look, I just didn't, all right? There's a big difference between doing number one and doing number two in someone's bowl, is what I mean to say."

"The only difference is in your head, Brutus," said Harriet. "And you know why? Because you have no respect for me, that's why."

"I have all the respect in the world for you, sugar plum. Absolutely. I just never thought—"

"I'd find out?"

"—I'd suffer an accident like that."

"And how many times did you suffer this 'accident?'" she asked, making air quotes.

"Um…" He shot a quick glance in my direction and I held up a single digit. "Um…" I stressed the digit with a pointed look in his direction. "Um… maybe like… six times?"

"Six times!"

Oh, dear. Now he'd gone and done it.

"You peed in my bowl *six times?*"

"Well, no. Like I said, I always tried to be fair and share the, um…"

"Fruits of your labor. I see. So you peed in my bowl twice, in Dooley's bowl twice and in Max's bowl also twice, is that it?"

"It could have been less… or more. I didn't exactly keep count."

Oh, dear, oh, dear, oh, dear.

"Right!" Harriet got up and walked off. And when Brutus made to follow her, she said, "No, Brutus. You're in the doghouse from now on. So please stay right where you are."

"But—"

But Harriet held up her paw. "Talk to the paw, Brutus.

Talk to the paw." And then she was gone, presumably to take a long hard long sniff at her water bowl *and* her kibble bowl, to determine whether Brutus had or had not relieved himself there.

"I told you specifically to tell her you only had that mishap once!" I told Brutus.

"Oh, is that why you held up one claw?"

"Yes, Brutus. That was why I held up one claw. One, as in: one lapse of judgment on your part—not six!"

"I only did it once," said Dooley. "And look where it got me."

"Dooley, did Gran have the talk with you yet?" I asked.

"What talk?"

"You'll see." I turned back to Brutus. "Look, buddy, you *have* to tell Harriet it only happened once, and even then you peed in your *own* bowl, *not* hers. It's important."

"Why? You think she'll stay mad at me if I don't?"

"Oh, yes, she will. She'll stay mad at you pretty much for the rest of your natural life, and possibly even long after that —haunting you in the afterlife."

"Oh, boy," he said with a sigh as he placed his head on his paws. "I should have known it was a bad idea. I just figured a little pre-tinkle wouldn't hurt anyone, you know. Seeing as there are so many people that drink their own pee and seem to like it."

This had Dooley look up in surprise. "People drink their own pee?"

"Oh, sure. Some guy called Gandhi used to drink his own pee all the time, or so I'm told. He swore by it. And plenty of others, too, and they think it's just the greatest thing."

"But why?" asked Dooley. Clearly this wasn't something he'd seen on the Discovery Channel yet.

"They claim numerous health benefits—too numerous for me to name them."

"You mean you didn't pay attention," I said.

"Yeah there's that," he admitted. "Look, I can't just tell Harriet that I made a mistake and in fact only peed once, and in my own bowl at that. She'll never believe me now."

"Then I'll tell her."

He gave me a skeptical look. "She'll just think you're trying to cover for me."

"Brilliant, Brutus! That's brilliant!" I said.

"What is?"

"Never mind. I know exactly what to say to make this whole thing go away."

And with these words, I trotted off in Harriet's wake, leaving Brutus and Dooley to stare after me in wonder.

15

"Look, I promise you that's how it went down," I told Harriet. "Don't you believe me?" I added with an incredulous little laugh.

"So you expect me to believe that *you're* actually the one who peed in my bowl, and when you told Brutus he decided to take the rap for your mishap and fessed up instead?"

"That's how it happened," I said with a shrug. "Brutus immediately understood you'd be very upset, and since he didn't want two of his best friends to be mad at each other, he told me he'd tell you he'd done it instead."

"Oh, Max. It's very sweet of you to try and get Brutus off the hook and all, but—"

"I'm not trying to get Brutus off the hook!" I cried. "I accidentally peed in your bowl, and when I told him he said, 'I'll take care of it, Max,' and that's the God's honest truth!"

She studied me for a moment. "Either you're a much better liar than I always thought you were, or this really happened."

"Trust me, it happened," I said, and projected my most honest face. It was important I healed this rift between the two partners, as I could sense that Harriet, who is just about the most prissy cat I know, would never tolerate this kind of abuse of her personal hygiene by her partner. From me she might—just might—accept it. Maybe.

"I don't know," she said finally. "I find it hard to believe you would have an 'accident' on your way to your litter box and decide to relieve yourself in my bowl—*my* bowl!"

"Look, I already explained to you how I thought it was my bowl, and I only saw it was yours after I'd already done the deed. And I promise you that as soon as I realized what had happened, I told Marge, and she threw out the contaminated water and replaced it with fresh water from the tap."

"So you promise me I never drank from your..." She made a disgusted face. "... whatever?"

"I promise you that the stuff never touched your lips, Harriet."

"Mh." She thought for a moment, then said, "Pinky swear?"

"Pinkie swear," I said with a smile, and as soon as I held up my pinkie, I felt a giant load fall from my back.

Just then, Brutus and Dooley walked in, and Brutus said, "Dooley has something he wants to confess, Harriet."

"It was me," said Dooley mournfully. "I peed in your bowl, not Brutus. And when I told him what I'd done he said he'd take the blame."

Have you ever watched a volcano right before it erupts? It's not a pretty sight. Steam rises up from its innards, and you just know it's going to explode any moment, and you're going to get pummeled with pieces of hot lava and rocks and that famous pyroclastic cloud that moves at 400 miles an hour and destroys everything in its wake.

Well, just such a moment had now arrived, only the volcano was Harriet, and even though the warning signs were all there, Brutus gave her a look of such inanity that he reminded me of how the inhabitants of Pompeii must have looked just before they got the boiling contents of Mount Vesuvius dumped in their unsuspecting necks.

So I decided I'd better run for cover, and as I passed Dooley, I grabbed his paw and steered him in the direction of the pet flap.

And we'd only just left Marge and Tex's kitchen when the eruption began.

I can promise you it wasn't pretty.

"Why did you go and do that for?" I asked as soon as we were out of earshot.

"Do what for?" asked Dooley innocently.

"Take the blame for Brutus's mistake."

"Well, he asked me to. He suddenly got the idea and asked me to tell Harriet what I just told her."

"Oh, dear," I said. I probably should have included Brutus and Dooley in my plans, and laid it all out for them in the minutest detail for the meanest intelligence to understand. But I'd wanted to catch Harriet before she disappeared, and that was my fatal mistake.

Now she wouldn't merely be upset with Brutus, but with me and Dooley, too, for trying to deceive her.

"Dooley?" suddenly asked Gran as we passed the table of adults. "A word, please?"

So I left Dooley in Grandma's care, while I went off in search of some peace and quiet. I needed to think up a new strategy on how to deal with Harriet's latest eruption. The future of our friendly foursome depended on it.

And I'd just entered the house when I came upon Dudley Checkers, wandering around Odelia's living room, and looking at picture frames and generally making himself right at home—in a house that technically wasn't his.

"Oh, hi there," he said when he saw me. "Max, is it?" He

crouched down and tickled me under the chin. "Why, aren't you a chunky kitty?"

I frowned at the guy. I don't like to be called chunky. I mean, can I help it that I was born with big bones?

"So where are your friends, Max?" he asked. "Oh, that's right. You divide your time between Odelia's place and her parents'. Yeah, she told me all about you and your little buddies. She also told me you had a big scare this morning. Some crazy person tried to set you on fire." He shook his head. "Personally I think crimes against pets are the worst crimes imaginable. Right up there with crimes against kids. But then that's me. I'm a big pet fan myself." He then gave me a big smile and tickled me behind the ears and got up.

I don't know why, but I was already starting to like this kid. I mean, anyone who loves cats is all right in my book, you know.

Odelia then walked in, followed by Chase. "Oh, I see you've met Max," said Odelia.

"Yeah, he's a big cutie, isn't he?" said Dudley.

"Yeah, we think so," said Odelia.

For a moment an awkward silence ensued, the kind of awkward silence that tends to exist between a brother and a sister who've never met before and didn't even know the other one existed until now. Then Odelia laughed an awkward little laugh, and so did Dudley, and then Chase said, "I have to tell you, Dudley, that the story you told us at dinner really got me, man. Your mom dying and you finding your dad and all? Heavy."

"Thanks, Chase. I'm just glad I finally got to meet you guys. It's just… I grew up thinking I was an only child, you know. And now suddenly… I've got a sister!"

Chase tapped his chest with his fist for some reason, and said, "And a brother, too, buddy," then clasped the other guy in a tight embrace. There was a lot of back-slapping, and

Odelia, wiping away a tear, watched the emotional scene, sniffling all the while.

And then she joined the group hug. And since I didn't want to be left behind, I joined in, too.

What can I say? It's one thing to see this stuff in a Lifetime movie, but something else to be suddenly right in the middle of it. And I may even have shed a happy tear, too.

16

"Look, Dooley," said Gran. "Sometimes people make mistakes, and that's only natural. And sometimes cats make mistakes, and that's okay, too. If they own up to those mistakes, and are honest about them and apologize, you will generally discover that your friends and your loved ones will find it in their hearts to forgive and forget."

Dooley looked up at Gran, and said, "But what if the mistake is so big that they can't forgive and forget, Gran?"

"Oh, Dooley," said Gran, placing a hand on the small cat's head. "Your mistake was a very small one, darling. In fact I don't even think it can be called a mistake at all. I'd call it an accident. And who can blame you for an accident, right?"

"You mean… Max will be able to forgive and forget?"

"I talked to Max, and he's already forgiven you, and he probably would have forgotten about it, too, if you didn't keep reminding him."

"Oh," said Dooley, taking all this in. It was some really heady stuff, he thought, all this talk of forgiving and forgetting. "You know, Gran, I think that maybe you're right."

"Of course I'm right. Have you ever known me not to be

right?"

He preferred not to answer that, but instead said, "You see, Brutus did the exact same thing as me. He also had an accident. Or in fact he had six accidents."

"What do you mean?"

"Well, he just confessed that he peed in all of our bowls on six separate occasions, and now Harriet is very angry with him, because Brutus asked me to tell Harriet that it had in fact been me who'd been peeing in her bowl, but since Max had already told her it had been him, now she's even more angry than before."

Gran chuckled at this for a reason that Dooley couldn't quite comprehend, but then he already knew from extensive experience that sometimes humans laughed at different things than cats, and that was all right with him.

"Looks like I'll have to have a word with Harriet too," she said. "Though I think I'll wait until she's cooled down some."

"So you think Max isn't angry with me anymore?"

"Sweetie, Max was never angry with you to begin with."

"Oh," he said, and a warm glow suddenly expanded right across his chest. "That's a big relief, Gran. That means I can probably start drinking water again."

"What do you mean, you silly cat?" she cried. "You haven't stopped drinking because of this thing, have you?" He gave her a sheepish look, and she laughed again. "Here, take this," she said, and handed him her glass of water. "And I want to see you drink, you hear?"

So he drank, and then drank some more, and when the glass was half empty, Gran urged him to drink even more, and so he did.

It tasted good. And he was almost sure there was no pee involved this time. At least that's what he hoped.

I was just about to head on out to cat choir when Odelia stopped me in my tracks. "Oh, no, you don't," she said.

"What do you mean?" I asked.

"Where are you going?"

"Cat choir."

"There's a dangerous cat killer out there, Max, so I want you to stay inside tonight—and every other night until this guy is caught."

"But it's cat choir. I have to go."

"No, you don't."

And then I gave her the kind of look only cats can muster. It requires a lot of practice, but I think I must have nailed it, for she said, "Oh, don't give me that puss-in-boots look, you."

"But it's cat choir," I said imploringly. "I want to go see my friends."

"All right," she said finally. "But on one condition and one condition only."

"Anything," I said.

Oh, boy. I probably shouldn't have said that.

"*I*s he really going to follow us around everywhere we go from now on?" asked Harriet annoyedly.

"Yeah, that's the condition," I said.

We all glanced back at Chase, who was following us from a safe distance. He looked as annoyed as Harriet, or maybe even more so.

Odelia had told us not to engage with Chase, as he was going to try and catch this cat killer in the act, and so we had to lure the killer out so Chase could catch him unawares.

"I'm not sure Shanille will like this," said Brutus. "She

usually doesn't allow humans."

He was right. Cats usually don't allow humans at their secret gatherings, and so Chase was in for a surprise: he would be the first human ever to attend cat choir. Not that the cop was looking forward to it, judging from the sour expression on his face.

"Why is he keeping his head down like that?" asked Dooley.

"Because he doesn't want to be seen by the cat killer," said Brutus.

"Or his colleagues," I ventured. Odelia had told me Chase felt very nervous about being spotted by his colleagues whilst on cat guard duty. He apparently found it beneath himself, a homicide cop, to have to guard his girlfriend's four cats. And he was afraid that if his colleagues caught him at it, they would start rolling around on the floor laughing.

He probably had a point.

"I think it's going to be fun," said Brutus. "Chase could even join in with the singing."

"If you think this is going to be fun you've got another thing coming, Brutus," said Harriet, who clearly hadn't forgiven her mate. "Or you, Max. Or even you, Dooley."

"What did I do?" asked Dooley, surprised.

"You lied to me—Brutus asked you to lie and so you did. And now I'm never going to be able to trust you again. Ever."

"But why?" asked Dooley.

"Because you lied!"

"No, I didn't."

"Yes, you did. You said it was you who peed in my bowl and it wasn't."

"But I was only trying to help Brutus."

"Oh, Dooley," said Harriet with a sigh. "Okay, so maybe I can forgive you. After all, you are a very naive cat, and I can see you meant no harm. But you, Max, I will never forgive."

"I was only trying to stop you guys from breaking up," I argued. "I hate it when you fight, and so I figured I might as well give it a shot."

"Well, you shouldn't have. In fact I want you to promise me you'll never interfere in my love life again. Is that understood?"

"Yes, Harriet," I said dutifully.

"Fine. Okay, so I can forgive you, too, Max, for you were only trying to help. But you, Brutus, I will never, ever be able to forgive you—ever! Is that understood?"

"But it was an accident," argued the butch black cat.

"Six times is no accident, Brutus. In fact I'm starting to think you did it on purpose."

"Why would I pee in your bowl on purpose?"

"I don't know—because you're weird like that?"

"I'm not weird like that!"

"Well, obviously you are, or else you wouldn't have peed in my bowl—six times!"

I decided to leave Harriet and Brutus at it. Frankly I wasn't all that keen on being in the middle of this lovers' tiff anymore, and I already regretted having interfered.

And as Harriet and Brutus went this way, I decided to take the long way to the park, Dooley in my wake.

But that obviously didn't sit well with Chase, who immediately came jogging up behind us and bodily picked us both up, then set us down again next to Harriet and Brutus, who hadn't stopped arguing and hadn't even noticed we'd briefly left.

"You guys have to stay together," growled Chase. "Odelia's orders."

Oh, darn it. And to think I thought having a human bodyguard would be fun. Clearly I'd been mistaken. And the worst part? We couldn't even talk to the guy!

17

When Chase had accepted the assignment he'd known it wasn't going to be a walk in the park, and now that he was walking in the park, trailing four cats on their way to something called 'cat choir,' he was already feeling the strain.

As a rule he was more of a dog person, though he'd come to like and appreciate his girlfriend's cats in the time he'd spent with them. But still. Having to spend the night looking after four felines while they gathered with dozens of other felines in a park?

Not exactly his idea of a good time!

And so when he finally reached the playground, he was surprised to find that there were so many more cats than he'd anticipated. There were cats all over that jungle gym, cats in the sandbox, cats on the swing, cats on the seesaw and cats on the slide. In fact there were cats everywhere he looked, and they all seemed to be looking at him, too.

And then there was the meowing. Oh, dear Lord, there was so much meowing going on, and mewling, and mewing, and even caterwauling.

It was frankly a little disconcerting to realize that there existed this entire cat population in Hampton Cove that he hadn't fully been aware of until now.

Max, Dooley, Harriet and Brutus seemed a lot more relaxed about the prospect of encountering this many felines than he was: they mingled with the others, and soon he couldn't even make out where they'd gone off to. They'd disappeared in a sea of fur.

So he simply took a seat on one of the benches placed there for the moms and dads watching their kids play, and thought that any would-be cat killer would have to be seriously suicidal to try and attack the cats on their own turf, where they were clearly in the majority, and would stand no nonsense.

His phone chimed and he picked it out of his pocket. "Hey, babe," he said.

"And? How are you holding up, Mr. Catsitter?"

"Frankly, babe? I don't think your cats need a catsitter at all. There's so many cats here this cat killer would have to be absolutely crazy to try and attack them."

"I still appreciate you watching out for them. Oh, and watch out for the…"

Just at that moment the caterwauling had reached a crescendo, and he couldn't make out what Odelia was saying. It sounded a lot like 'shoes,' which of course was just nuts.

But just then, completely out of the blue, a shoe struck him in the head, and he grunted with dismay. The shoe dropped into his lap and he saw that it was an old shoe, and a sturdy one, too.

"What the…" he muttered as he picked it up and studied it. And that's when a second shoe hit him in the chest. "Oh, for crying out loud!" he said, and got up, glancing around. And then he saw it: in one of the houses facing the park the lights had come on, and an irate citizen was screaming, "Damn cats with your damn screaming every damn night!"

Yep. This was going to be a looooong night.

§⋅

*P*oor Chase was being pummeled by one of our regulars. There are people in this world who appreciate art, and then there are the cultural barbarians, who hate it. And it was just our rotten luck that the park where we like to practice our art is surrounded by these cultural barbarians, who choose to express their disapproval of our nocturnal activities by throwing shoes and other objects in our direction.

I've long since passed the moment where I truly care about this peculiar human habit, but obviously Chase, being subjected to this abuse for the very first time, was shocked to be on the receiving end of several items of footwear.

Although in actual fact it had happened before, and in our own backyard, no less, where our next-door neighbor Kurt Mayfield is also a very avid shoe thrower.

Chase now stood shaking his fist at the irate homeowners who stood shaking their fists at us. All in all, the cop wasn't having a good time, I could tell. And I felt for him.

"Maybe we should tell Odelia to call off this guard duty thing," I suggested now.

"But what if the cat killer strikes again?" said Dooley. "I feel much safer knowing Chase is right there keeping an eye on us, Max."

"Yeah, I guess you're right." I felt much safer, too.

"I think Chase should do this all the time," said Harriet. "I've always wanted my own bodyguard. Makes me feel like a real star. Like Kim Kardashian or Gwyneth Paltrow."

I'm not sure Chase would enjoy the prospect of being

reduced to mere guard duty, on the same level as Kim or Gwyneth's bodyguards, but then the man couldn't understand what we said, so it wasn't as if he'd ever know.

"I think it's great," said Brutus. "And in fact I think this guard duty should probably be expanded. No man can guard us twenty-four-seven hours all by his lonesome. It takes at least two guards to do the job the way it's supposed to be done. Or maybe even four, as no guard worth his or her salt likes to do this alone. Two teams of two guards is what this job requires, and so I'm going to tell Odelia she should recruit three more cops."

"I doubt whether Uncle Alec will agree," I said. "His cops probably have more important things to do than to guard Odelia's cats all the time."

"What could be more important than making sure that we're safe?" asked Harriet, and I had the impression the question was a rhetorical one, so I didn't answer.

Kingman, who's one of our best friends and also our local cat population's unofficial mayor, came waddling over. He's a very large cat, and contrary to myself doesn't have his big bones to blame for his sizable form.

"What's your human doing here?" he asked, casting curious glances at Chase, who'd taken a seat on his bench again, but was eyeing the shoe thrower with a kindling eye.

"We were in the attic this morning and then we were locked up inside a box and then the box was set on fire with us still in it, and even though we did a lot of spitting and licking that didn't help," said Dooley, causing Kingman to frown and turn to me.

"What is he talking about?"

"A cat killer attacked us this morning," I said. "He tried to set us on fire."

"Oh, my God. And how did you survive?"

I told him the whole story, and Kingman was properly impressed.

"So Odelia assigned us a bodyguard," said Harriet proudly. "And soon she'll probably assign us a couple more. We are VICs, after all."

"I'm afraid to ask, but what is a VIC?" asked Kingman.

"A Very Important Cat," said Harriet, then walked off to socialize with her friends.

"Odelia is also going to organize training for us," I said.

"Like dog training?"

Kingman made a face. "That doesn't sound like a lot of fun. Better you than me, Max."

"Yeah, I'm not exactly looking forward to it either," I confessed.

"You know what you should do? Hire a watchcat instead of this human of yours."

"What do you mean?" asked Dooley.

"You know, like a watchdog, but a feline one."

"I didn't even know watchcats existed."

"Oh, sure." He glanced at Chase again. "You better give it some thought. I mean, it's really awkward for a cat to be guarded by a human. Not dignified."

I saw what he meant. Cats are the kind of pets that are known far and wide for being able to take care of themselves. We've never needed a human to take care of us before, and it frankly was humiliating to have Chase tagging along wherever we went.

"That's so kind of you, Kingman," said Dooley. "You would really be our watchcat? Guard us with your life?"

"Me? Are you nuts? I was thinking of Clarice. She's easily Hampton Cove's toughest cat—her reputation precedes her. I'll bet that if she took you under her paw, no cat killer would dare to come near you again."

"Clarice would never take the job," said Brutus.

"Why not? Everyone can be bought, Brutus, even Clarice."

But Brutus was shaking his head. "Not Clarice. She's a free cat, and would never accept payment in exchange for her services."

"Look, my human has just managed to land himself a date with the most gorgeous female I've ever seen. And why do you think that is? Because Wilbur owns a business, and even gorgeous females are susceptible to the siren song of the good old moolah."

We all stared at the big cat in shock. Wilbur Vickery isn't exactly Hampton Cove's most eligible bachelor. In fact he's probably our town most ineligible bachelor. And to think that he managed to snag a date with a woman was… surprising, to say the least.

"Just ask her," Kingman suggested. "I'm sure you'll be able to come to some sort of an understanding."

It was an avenue worth pursuing I had to agree. Clarice is a feral cat, and as such probably the most intimidating cat in all of Hampton Cove. If she were to guard us around the clock, no wannabe cat killer would get close to us ever again.

"All right," I said therefore. "It's worth a shot."

"She'll never do it," Brutus insisted. "Never."

"Maybe if we ask her nicely?" Dooley suggested.

"Mark my words," said Brutus. "She'll laugh in your face, Max."

Just then, Chase came wandering over, clearly bored after having spent the past half hour on that hard wooden bench. "Just out of curiosity, Max," said the cop. "How long do these recitals usually go on for?"

I smiled up at the cop, and held up three digits.

He groaned. "Three hours? You've got to be kidding me."

I shook my head. Nope. I wasn't kidding.

"See?" said Kingman. "You need a cat to watch your back.

Only a cat can endure cat choir without wanting to jump off a bridge."

And with a loud guffaw, he waddled off again.

"Poor Chase," said Dooley. "He looks very unhappy, doesn't he, Max?"

"Yeah, he does. Maybe Kingman is right. Guarding cats is not a human's job."

We all watched as Chase slouched back to his bench, looking distinctly unhappy with the fate life had dealt him.

And so I swore that tomorrow I'd look up Clarice and offer her a deal. Free kibble for life and free fresh water.

And now I just had to convince Brutus not to pee in Clarice's bowl.

Or any bowl, for that matter.

18

"This is pretty pointless if you ask me," said Scarlett.

"Nobody asked you so be quiet," riposted Vesta.

"I think Scarlett is right," said Father Reilly. "Just driving around like this doesn't seem to make any sense."

"Driving around like this keeps the bad guys away," said Vesta.

"I don't see any bad guys," said Wilbur Vickery. "Do you see any bad guys, Francis?"

"No, I don't," said Father Reilly, craning his neck as he glanced around.

"That's because we're patrolling," said Vesta. "If we weren't patrolling these streets they'd be crawling with bad guys. It's just like the light in the fridge, see."

"The light in the fridge?" asked Scarlett, looking at her as if she'd just lost her mind.

"You don't see the light going out in the fridge, do you? Because the light only goes out when you close the door, and when you open the door to look, it flashes on again. And then when you close the door, it goes out—BUT YOU DON'T KNOW IT GOES OUT!"

Vesta's fellow watch members were quiet for a moment, as they considered this intriguing piece of information, then Father Reilly said, "So in this comparison, the bad guys are the light in the fridge? Or the bad guys are the lack of light in the fridge?"

"Oh, who cares!" said Vesta as she took a turn. They were cruising along the quiet and deserted streets of their neighborhood in her little red Peugeot, and she suddenly wished she'd be able to buy the watch a proper car, just like she'd already told Scarlett about a million times. A nice big car. A van or maybe even one of them fancy Escalades. A car that made the bad guys quake in their boots when they saw them coming.

Father Reilly yawned. "How long do you want to keep doing this, Vesta? I need to get up early. I have a sermon to write."

"So you actually write your own sermons?" asked Scarlett. "I always thought you made those up on the spot."

"No, I write all of my sermons," said the priest, a little stung by this comment. "And it's hard work, too, as I have to insert small passages from the Scriptures."

"Just download that stuff from the internet," grunted Wilbur. "Plenty of sermons there."

"I am not going to download my sermons off the internet," said Father Reilly. "My parishioners—"

"Your parishioners would never know the difference," argued the shopkeeper.

"Well, I beg to differ," said the father a little haughtily.

"Look," said Vesta suddenly as she pointed at a nearby shrub.

"Buxus Semptervirens," said Father Reilly, nodding appreciatively. "Also known as Boxwood. I instructed the church gardener to plant it in our church garden. A very hardy plant. It likes its soil to be kept moist but—"

"I'm not talking about the plant, you old fool," said Vesta. "I'm talking about the guy hiding behind it!"

They all stared intently at the Boxwood now, and lo and behold, suddenly a face emerged from behind the shapely shrub, lit up by the high beam of Vesta's aged little car.

"Let's go get him!" Scarlett cried excitedly.

So the members of the watch all got out of the car and descended upon the scene, eager to bag their first bad guy for the night.

Vesta had taken her deceased ex-husband's old shotgun from the garden shed, Scarlett was carrying a stun gun, Father Reilly had brought a billy club, and Wilbur? He'd brought along the baseball bat he liked to keep next to the cash register at the store.

The hoodlum, when they approached him, didn't even attempt to make a run for it. Instead he simply cowered in fear and cried, "Please don't hurt me. You can take everything I have but please don't hurt me—I have a wife and kids—and a dog!"

Vesta frowned at the man. "Ted? What the hell are you doing out here in the middle of the night?"

For it was indeed Ted Trapper, her very own neighbor.

"Vesta? Is that you?" the mild-mannered accountant asked, his voice betraying his extreme elation. "I thought you were a couple of gangsters eager to hit on me."

"We're not gangsters, Ted," said Scarlett. "We're your neighborhood watch, here to protect you from harm. Make sure you feel safe at all times."

Ted, who didn't look like he felt safe at all, nodded a few times in quick succession. "Oh, hello, Father Reilly—I hadn't seen you there. Wilbur."

"Hello, Ted," said Father Reilly warmly. "We're very sorry for scaring you like that."

"It's fine," said Ted, getting up with a little help from the good priest. "I couldn't sleep so I figured I might as well take Rufus for a walk." He gestured to the shrub, where his big sheepdog Rufus now came peeping out—he looked as terrified as his owner.

"Great watchdog you've got there, Ted," said Wilbur with a grin.

"Yeah, Rufus isn't exactly the world's greatest hero," said Ted as he called his dog to him and Rufus now reluctantly appeared. He sniffed Vesta's hand, then in turn sniffed Father Reilly, Wilbur and Scarlett, before sinking down onto his haunches, his tail happily wagging and giving an excited bark. The watch had been vetted and approved.

"What a waste of time," said Vesta once they were back inside the vehicle and cruising those Hampton Cove mean streets once more. "That's what I mean about getting ourselves some designated wheels for the watch. Then when people see us coming they'll know it's us and wouldn't feel the need to go and hide in the bushes."

"And who's going to pay for this designated set of wheels?" asked Scarlett.

"Not me," said Wilbur. As a Main Street shopkeeper he was being solicited for all kinds of projects all the time, and he'd long ago learned always to say no, lest his meager profit margins were eroded even more.

"And not me, either," said Father Reilly when all eyes turned to him. "Contrary to what you might think being a local church leader isn't the road to riches."

"Yeah, and my pension doesn't stretch that far either," said Scarlett.

"I thought you were going to ask your son for one of his squad cars?" said Wilbur.

"I asked and he said no," said Vesta. "Says cop cars are for cops only. Silly rule."

They were silent for a moment, as the Peugeot's ancient engine cozily prattled on.

"Oh, I've got an idea!" Vesta suddenly exclaimed as she slapped the steering wheel.

"Uh-oh," said Scarlett, earning herself a nasty glance from her friend.

"Why don't we ask my son's new girlfriend?"

"Charlene? And why would the Mayor buy us a new car?"

"Because we're doing her a big favor, that's why. We're keeping her streets safe."

"Local government nowadays doesn't have any money to spare, I'm afraid," said Father Reilly with a sad shake of the head. "I asked the Mayor for money for a new church roof and she turned me down. Said I should ask my parishioners to chip in."

"That's it!" Vesta cried. "We'll start one of 'em online collections! Gofungus!"

"I think it's called Gofundus," said the priest with an indulgent smile.

"Go Fund *Me*," Wilbur corrected him. "We did one last year for my mom's new hip. We got enough for three hips, so my sister used the money for a new boob job instead."

"Do you really think people are going to give money for a new car for the watch?" asked Scarlett dubiously.

"Of course! Who doesn't like to live in a safe neighborhood? I'll get on it tomorrow morning first thing. And if we're not driving around in a fancy big Escalade this time next week I'll eat my hat."

"You don't have a hat," Wilbur pointed out.

"Then I'll eat your hat! Or Father Reilly's!"

"You can eat my hat," said Scarlett. "I was thinking of buying myself a new one anyway."

"Wise-ass," said Vesta with a grin, and suddenly the mood

in the car was uplifted to such a degree that for the rest of their patrol, a pleasant atmosphere reigned, and Father Reilly didn't even bring up the delicate and intricate art of sermon-writing again.

19

"Look, I don't want him here, all right?"

"But, honey!"

"No, you listen to me. How do you even know he's yours?"

A smile appeared on Marge's husband's face. "I just know he is. Besides, he looks exactly like me, doesn't he? He's my spitting image."

"No, he doesn't. He looks nothing like you."

They were in their bedroom, conducting a whispered conversation, which was outrageous enough if you thought about it: there they were, in their own house, having to whisper because suddenly Tex had gotten it into his nut to invite a complete stranger into their home—a complete stranger who claimed, without evidence, that he was his son!

"I didn't even know you dated Jaqlyn Checkers. You never told me!"

"I've been trying to remember. Before Dudley showed up I hadn't thought about Jaqlyn for over thirty years. I even had to look up her picture. And as far as I can remember we never really dated. We went out a couple of times, before she dumped me for Timothy Gass, who had really nice hair back in the day. And of course he had a car."

"But you do remember getting her pregnant," Marge said acerbically.

"No! I didn't think we ever got… that far." He blushed a little as he said it. "And she definitely never said anything about being pregnant. Though I seem to remember now that she dropped out of school the last semester of high school. The story back then was that her dad had gotten a post as ambassador to Italy. I hadn't even been aware he was a diplomat. Then again, I guess anyone can be an ambassador if they know the right people."

"She never told you about the baby?"

Tex shook his head. On his lap were their old photo albums, which he'd taken into his son's room so he could show him a little more about the family he'd suddenly found himself to be a member of.

"I find it very hard to believe you made this girl pregnant and you can't even remember, Tex. You weren't exactly the school Adonis back in the day."

"All I remember is that we fumbled around a little on the backseat of her dad's Volvo one night. Like I said, I don't remember going that far, but apparently we must have."

"Oh, Tex," said Marge. "For a doctor you're hopelessly clueless sometimes."

"Obviously I must have had relations with the woman, otherwise Dudley wouldn't have been born." He smiled. "I always wanted a son. I love Odelia, but a son is… special."

She gave him a dirty look which he totally didn't catch and folded her arms across her chest, giving herself up to dark thoughts about her husband and men in general. Why was it they all considered a son their highest goal?

"Dudley wants to be a doctor, you know," said Tex, with a beatific smile on his face. "Or at least he always wanted to be a doctor but his mom couldn't afford the tuition so he never pursued his dream. Maybe he still can. With a little help from his dear old dad."

"Oh, Tex!" Marge cried, and swung her feet from the bed. She couldn't stand to be in the same room with this man anymore.

"What did I say?" asked her husband dumbly.

But she was already stalking out of the room and then she was stomping down the stairs and into the kitchen. And she'd just taken the milk from the fridge so she could warm up a glass, when suddenly she became aware of a noise nearby and slammed the fridge door shut, only to be faced with… Dudley, staring at her intently!

"D-Dudley," she stuttered, much surprised. "You startled me."

"Oh, I'm sorry, Mrs. Poole," said Dudley in that obsequious and overly polite way of his. "I didn't mean to scare you. I just had one of those midnight cravings, you know." He smiled and gestured to the bottle of milk in her hand. "Like you, I guess."

"Yeah, I-I couldn't sleep, so I figured I might as well have a glass of warm milk."

"My mom used to drink warm milk before going to bed," said Dudley as he leaned against the kitchen counter. "With a spoon of honey and some nutmeg. Always did the trick. Even when she was sick, she used to ask me for a glass of warm milk." His smile faltered and Marge suddenly felt bad for talking about the kid behind his back. He clearly had been through a terrible time with his mother dying from cancer.

"I'm so sorry," she said. "That must have been really hard on you. To lose your mom like that."

"It was," he said, then his smile returned. "That's why I'm so happy to have found Tex—and you, Mrs. Poole. A new start for me. A new chance at happiness."

She nodded, and poured some milk in a pan and put it on the stove then pressed the designated spot on the ceramic cooktop to turn up the heat. The cooktop instantly glowed hot.

"I can't wait to get to know you better, Mrs. Poole," said Dudley as he dragged a casual hand through his neat blond-do. "You, my dad, Vesta… and Odelia, of course—my sister."

"You can call me Marge, Dudley," she said as she took two cups from the cupboard.

"Thanks, Marge."

"Did your mother never mention Tex before?"

Dudley shook his head. "No, and she was very sorry that she hadn't. At the end she said she wished she'd been more honest with me. I could have had a real father in my life much sooner. Which is why I'm so happy that you invited me to stay. This way I can make up for lost time."

"That's nice," Marge muttered vaguely.

"You know what? Maybe we can all do something together tomorrow. Like… going to the beach? Or see a movie together as a family?"

Marge made a noncommittal noise. She wasn't really ready for family trips with this kid yet, but couldn't exactly come right out and tell him so.

She poured the milk into the cups and handed him one.

"If the death of my mother taught me one thing, it's that you have to enjoy every day as if it's the last one. Spend time with your family while you can, for you never know when it will be over. And it can all be over like that." He snapped his fingers, startling her.

She put a hand on her heart and laughed. "I'm sorry. I guess I'm a little on edge."

"And why is that, Marge?" he asked, leaning closer until they were almost face to face. "You're not scared of me, are you?"

"No–no, of course not."

"I mean, I can see how this might look to you: your husband inviting a stranger into your home. Who knows where I've been—what I've been up to, you know?"

She stared at him. There was a strange glow in the kid's eyes. A glow she didn't know how to interpret. It was almost… menacing.

But then he flashed that engaging smile again, and said, "I'm off to bed, Marge. I hope you have a nice evening."

"Yeah. You, too," she said, and returned his smile. But as soon as he was gone, her smile faltered, and she wondered who this kid was.

20

"I find that very hard to believe, honey. Tex? Owner of a plot of land on Grover's Point?"

"That's what those developers told me. And if he doesn't sell them his little piece of land they can't proceed with their plans to build that mall."

"The Charlene Butterwick Mall," Alec said with a grin.

"The Butterwick Mall," she corrected him, and playfully tapped him on the nose. They were in bed, the television softly playing in a corner of the room, and talking about how their day had been.

Both Charlene and Alec had a habit of going to bed late, and getting up early. Hard-working professionals, both of them, they didn't get a lot of sleep during the week.

"I'll have to ask him," said Alec. "But it would surprise me that my sister and her husband would have bought a piece of land without telling me."

"Maybe it belonged to Tex's parents?" Charlene suggested.

"Could be," he allowed. "But that still doesn't explain why

he doesn't want to sell. Unless they're not offering him enough."

"Oh, they're offering him plenty. In fact he can pretty much ask what he wants at this stage."

"So you've decided then? The mall is happening?"

"It's not up to me," she said, lying back against her fluffed-up pillow. "I've asked for a special council meeting to discuss the matter. I hope the other council members will offer some good feedback. And of course all kinds of studies will need to be done. Environmental impact report, social assessment… Then the Planning and Zoning Commission will take a whack at it, we'll set up meetings with the local community…"

"But the final decision is up to you?"

"As the Mayor my opinion carries a certain weight, sure."

He shook his head. "I wouldn't want to be in your shoes. Tough decision to make. If you say yes to the mall, shopkeepers and small business owners will be up in arms, and if you say no, plenty of locals will claim you're standing in the way of progress."

"Yeah, I know. Either way it won't be easy." She patted his big belly. "But let's not talk about work, shall we? I get enough of that at the office. When I'm home with you I want to do other things." And she wiggled her eyebrows meaningfully.

Alec grinned. "Oh, honey, I thought you'd never ask."

We were returning from cat choir, Chase in tow, when suddenly the burly cop grunted, "Hang on a moment," and strode out in front of us, taking on a vigilant stance and glancing this way and that, as if he'd suddenly become aware of nefarious activities.

"What is it, Max?" asked Dooley, concern lacing his voice.

"I don't know, Dooley," I said. "But it looks like Chase has seen or heard something."

Which would frankly surprise me, as the ears of a cat are usually a lot better at picking up signs of danger than human ears. Then again, Chase is no ordinary human. He's a cop who used to be in the NYPD, one of the country's better-trained police forces.

"I think it's the cat killer," said Brutus as we all anxiously followed Chase's every move. He was rooting through the bushes lining the sidewalk now, as if trying to catch whoever was lurking there, intent on causing us harm.

"I'm so glad Odelia asked Chase to be our bodyguard," said Harriet. "Life is so much harder without your own personal bodyguard. In fact I think I'll ask her to put Chase in charge of my bodyguard detail on a full-time basis from now on."

"Chase has a day job, Harriet," I pointed out. "You can't expect him to guard us day and night."

"Oh, yes, I can. And I'm sure he'd do it, too. He's Odelia's boyfriend, after all, so he has to do what she says."

"Um… it's not the job of a boyfriend to do everything his girlfriend says," I pointed out.

"Yes, it is," said Harriet, wide-eyed at my lack of understanding. "Of course it is."

"No, it isn't. Being a boyfriend isn't like being at someone's every beck and call, Harriet."

"Yes, it is," she said. "Isn't that right, twinkle toes?"

"Um…" said Brutus. Clearly he hadn't read the fine print when he'd signed up for boyfriend duty, for he looked a little stunned at Harriet's interpretation of the tasks of a boyfriend.

"Look, I'm a princess, Max," said Harriet, deciding to put me straight once and for all. "And every princess has a prince to look after her. And it's the prince's duty, but also his honor and his pleasure, to take care of his princess. Simple."

"I very much doubt whether Chase would agree with you," I said. "Or Odelia, for that matter."

"Oh, of course they agree with me. Everybody knows this, Max, except you, of course. Which is probably why you've never been able to find yourself a girlfriend."

I let the words hang in the air for a moment before replying. "I don't have a girlfriend because I haven't met the right one yet," I said. "Not because I'm not willing to enter into indentured servitude, like you seem to expect from your boyfriends."

"Oh, Max," she said with a little sigh. "You just don't get it, do you? And I'm starting to believe that you never will. Please explain it to him, Brutus. Or you know what? Maybe don't bother. He won't understand. Some cats never do."

And with these words, she turned away from me, as if the mere act of talking to me had drained her.

Well, it certainly made me tired arguing with her, let me tell you. But luckily at that moment Chase returned from his sojourn in the bushes, and said, "All clear! Move out!"

And so move out we did, like the obedient little platoon we were.

This time Chase led the way, Brutus and Harriet right behind him, and Dooley and I picking up the rear.

"Do you think Harriet is right, Max?" asked Dooley. "That the reason we don't have a girlfriend is because we don't understand girls and we never will?"

"No, I don't think Harriet is right at all, Dooley. The purpose of a boyfriend is not to cater to his girlfriend's every whim. At its core a relationship should be built on friendship, love and trust, not servitude, like Harriet seems to think."

"Okay," said Dooley, thinking hard about my words. "But

when you love someone, you're willing to do everything for them, right?"

"I guess so," I said.

"So maybe that's what Harriet means?"

I hadn't looked at it that way, but it seemed highly unlikely. Then again, I frankly had enough on my mind with this cat killer hanging around, and since I didn't want to get drawn into another fight with Harriet, I decided simply to drop the whole thing, and pretend the discussion had never even taken place.

21

When we finally arrived home we were met by Odelia, standing in the door. Next to her was… a dog.

"What's that?" I asked.

"That, my friend," said Brutus with a grin, "is what is commonly known as a dog. And in case you don't know what a dog is—a dog is a member of the canine species and…"

"I know what a dog is, Brutus. But what is it doing here?"

When we approached, Odelia waved at us and said, "I'm so glad you guys are all right."

"Of course they're all right, babe," said Chase, planting a quick kiss on her lips. "They've got the best cat bodyguard for miles around. Also the only cat bodyguard for miles around," he added a little ruefully.

"How did it go?" asked Odelia.

"Fine—if you can call a bunch of cats caterwauling all night fine."

She now crouched down and petted the big dog on the head. He was a dog of the Bulldog variety and was big and round and had one of those smushed-up faces that made it hard to know what he was thinking. His eyes were hooded, and saliva was dripping from twin pouches next to what I assumed was his mouth. He looked like someone had attempted to create a dog but hadn't entirely succeeded.

"Look, you guys," said Odelia. "Your knight in shining armor has arrived."

We all stared at her, then at the dog, not quite catching her drift.

"Rambo will be your guard dog from now on," she said. "I've got him on loan from the K9 squad. He's actually retired now, but still does odd jobs for them from time to time. In fact he's pretty much the K9 unit's mascot, so please be nice to him, all right?"

The dog, who hadn't spoken, now opened his mouth for the first time. I half expected more saliva to come pouring out, having been pooling up inside his mouth, but instead he said, in a deep rumbling voice, "Hi, cats."

"Hi... you," I said by way of greeting.

This was too much. A dog? Guarding cats? No way!

"Hi, Rambo," said Dooley, stepping to the fore. "Welcome to our humble home."

"Thanks, bud," said Rambo, not exactly conveying a wealth of emotion.

"This was my idea, you know," said Dooley proudly, and I gawked at him.

"Your idea!"

"Yeah, I thought a guard dog would make sure we don't get locked up and set on fire again."

"But... I thought you said we were going to get trained," I said to Odelia. "Like dogs!"

"No, I said I was going to get you a trained dog to look after you. And here he is. Yay!"

"Oh, dear Lord," I said. As if it wasn't enough to be

guarded by a human, now Odelia had to add a dog to the mix?

"I'm a great guard dog," said the dog. "I used to guard the president when he was in town."

"The president was in town?" I asked. "When was this? I must have missed it."

"What did he say?" asked Odelia, who can talk to cats, but unfortunately her abilities don't extend to dogs.

"He says he used to guard the president when he was in town."

"Oh, he probably means one of the former presidents," said Odelia.

"A former president!" I said. "How old are you!"

"Old," said the dog. "But that doesn't mean I've lost my bark." And to show us he meant what he said, he barked. Once.

Oh, dear. This was a disaster, wasn't it?

We all filed into the house, and soon Harriet and Brutus made themselves scarce, disappearing into the house next door. Dooley and I moved up the stairs and hopped onto the bed, waiting for Chase and Odelia to join us, and before I knew what was happening, suddenly a minor earthquake made the bed tremble and shake!

It was Rambo, making the great leap and following in our pawsteps.

And so when Odelia and Chase finally emerged, they found their bed bedecked not with holly, but with two members of the feline species and one, very large, drooling dog.

"I think we're going to need a bigger bed," said Chase, surveying the scene.

Somehow they managed to squeeze in, and soon Rambo was snoring away, showing us what a great guard dog he really was.

"I hope it wasn't too horrible?" said Odelia, addressing her boyfriend, not us.

"It was okay. I got hit with shoes all night, but apart from that it was all good."

"Oh, no. My poor baby."

"Poor cats. They have to go through this kind of thing all the time, I imagine."

"So many people out there who don't appreciate cats. I don't know what's going on with the world."

I could have told her: a distinct lack of aesthetic refinement. But I was on the verge of falling asleep, so I didn't bother.

"So now you have a brother, huh?" said Chase. "How does that feel?"

"I'm not sure. I guess it will take some getting used to."

"He seems like a great kid."

"Yeah, he seems really nice."

"Do you think he'll move in next door permanently?"

"I don't know. Mom doesn't seem all that happy with this new arrangement."

"I can imagine. It must have come as a great shock to her to discover that her husband fathered a son with another woman."

"Yeah, I better have a talk with her tomorrow. See how she's holding up."

They both lapsed into silence, then, and soon only soft snores could be heard—the snores of one woman (cute little snores), one male (as if he were trying to cut through a tree trunk), one canine (wet slobbering snores), and two felines (I can't tell you how that sounded because that's when I fell asleep).

22

"Max?"

"Mh?"

"Are you sure you told Rambo not to use our water bowls?"

We were staring at our water bowls, which were now absolutely devoid of water, but consisted instead of a generous helping of slobber. The same could be said for our kibble bowls, which had expertly been relieved of their contents, only traces of slop left. In fact all of the bowls were now empty, and the copious amounts of slop and slobber left no doubt as to the identity of the midnight marauder who'd performed this impressive feat.

"Odelia!" I bellowed. If there's one thing I'm very sensitive about it's of other pets eating my portion of kibble.

Odelia came staggering down the stairs, wearing an oversized sweater that clearly belonged to Chase, as it said 'I-heart-NYPD' and was rubbing her eyes. "What is it?" she murmured as she took a right turn into the kitchen, and almost slipped on a pool of drool. "Eek!" she said, lifting one bare foot to see what had attached itself there.

PURRFECT SON

"It's Rambo," I announced. "He's eaten all of our food."

"And drunk all of our water," Dooley added helpfully.

"And replaced same with a goodish pile of goo."

"Rambo!" said Odelia, then thunked her brow. "I totally forgot. Chase took him out for his morning walk."

"His morning walk?" I said. You must forgive me for not being better acquainted with the ways of the canine species. I've never lived with a dog before, you see, so this was definitely a first in every sense.

"Dogs go for a walk in the morning, Max," she explained. "That's how they get rid of their morning… doo-doo and wee-wee."

"Oh," I said, feeling silly. "Of course. I knew that."

Odelia stared down at the mess the old dog had made on the kitchen floor—and our neat row of bowls. "I gave him his own bowl of dog kibble," she said, pointing to a giant bowl that was, of course, empty. "Clearly it wasn't enough."

"He's a very large dog," I said. "He probably eats a lot."

"Maybe we should have a talk with him," Dooley suggested. "Teach him about the difference between mine and thine."

"Excellent idea, Dooley," I said. "I'm sure it was a simple misunderstanding that made him eat all of our food, and drink all of our water, too."

And since Odelia was going to be busy washing out our bowls—and scrubbing the kitchen floor—Dooley suggested we move next door for our first meal of the day.

We ambled into the backyard, then through the hedge and then in through the pet flap and into Marge and Tex's kitchen. When we arrived there we found Brutus and Harriet staring at their respective bowls, a look of distress on their faces.

"Someone ate all of our food," said Brutus.

"And drank all of our water," said Harriet.

"And left some kind of slime behind."

"I think it might have been aliens."

"Or ghosts," Brutus ventured. "Ghosts are always leaving some kind of slimy residue behind. It's called ectoplasm. That's how you can tell you've got ghosts."

"I can assure you it wasn't ghosts, and it wasn't aliens," I said.

"It was Rambo," Dooley said as he inspected his own bowl and sadly had to come to the conclusion that here, too, Rambo had eaten his fill, and had left nothing for us.

"Rambo did all this?" asked Harriet. "But that's impossible. No dog can possibly eat this much."

"He ate all the food next door, too," I said. "And if he'd had a third home to sneak into, I'm sure he'd have emptied the bowls there, too."

"This is too much!" said Harriet. "First Odelia hires a dog —a dog!—to guard us, and then the silly mutt eats all of our food!"

"At least he didn't pee in our bowls," I said with a pointed glance at Brutus. I still hadn't fully forgiven him for his midnight indiscretions.

"We're going to talk to him as soon as he gets back," Dooley announced.

"Wait, where is he?" asked Harriet.

"Out. Chase took him for a walk," I said.

"Out! So you're telling me both our canine *and* our human bodyguards left us all alone—exposed to who knows what kinds of dangers!"

"I'm sure this cat killer won't attack us when there's people around," I said.

"A bodyguard should be present at all times to guard your body," said Harriet decidedly. "What else are they there for?"

She had a point, I had to admit.

"He does have to do his business twice or three times a

day," I said. "That's how it works for dogs. And he can only do his business when he goes for a walk."

"Well, I for one don't feel safe," said Harriet. "And I want a different bodyguard. I want a human bodyguard. And I want him to be around twenty-four-seven. Who's with me?" And she held up her paw to indicate she wanted to put the matter to a vote.

Brutus immediately held up his paw, but I was reluctant to follow his example. "I don't know," I said. "I was going to talk to Clarice, and ask her to help us out, but we all know that will be a tough ask. And since we don't have any other options here... I say we keep Chase and we keep Rambo, at least if we can get him house-trained."

"Dooley? What say you?" Harriet snapped, giving me a fiery look that meant trouble.

"I'm with Max," said my friend.

"Of course you are," said Harriet. "Well, fine! I'll deal with this on my own. Come on, Brutus. Let's go."

"Go where?" asked Brutus.

"Out!" said Harriet, and stalked off.

Brutus gave us an apologetic grimace, then followed his girlfriend out through the pet flap.

"I wonder what she's going to do," said Dooley, as he thoughtfully studied his bowl, as if hoping that cat kibble would magically appear out of thin air. "Did you know that dogs could slobber this much, Max?"

"No, I didn't, Dooley."

He touched the goo with a look of distaste. "It feels like... the stuff they put on pies."

"I'm sure they don't put dog goo on pies."

And as we discussed the ins and outs of dog goo, suddenly Dudley came bounding down the stairs, looking distinctly cheerful. And why wouldn't he? He'd just found his long-lost dad—that he hadn't even known existed. Jerry

Springer, if he'd been present, would have handed him a fat contract on the spot.

"Hey, fellas," said the prodigal son when he spotted us. "What a lovely, lovely day this is, huh?"

And he opened the fridge and started rooting around as if this was his home—which I suppose now it was.

Next to come down the stairs, though she wasn't bounding but shuffling, was Gran. When she saw Dudley, she frowned. "So you're still here, huh?" she said, not sounding overly welcoming.

"Yup," said Dudley. "And can I just say, Mrs. Muffin, how very glad I am to meet you. My own grandmother died when I was three, and I always wanted to have a sweet old lady just like yourself to spend time with."

"For your information, sonny boy, I'm not an old lady. I'm only seventy-five. And secondly, if you think I'm going to spend time with you, you're delusional. I'm out of here." And to show Dudley she meant what she said, she promptly skedaddled.

"Not exactly the sweetest granny in the world, is she?" said Dudley, addressing us, I assumed, even though he wasn't looking at us but at Gran's disappearing back.

"Oh, Gran can be very sweet when she wants to be," I said. "But she can also be extremely testy."

"I guess I'll just have to win her over," said Dudley with a shrug, then took the box of cereal out of the cupboard and dumped a goodish helping into his mouth.

23

"Yeah, we bought that piece of land years ago, didn't we, hon? And for a bargain, too," said Tex as he poured some coffee for his guests—Charlene Butterwick and Alec.

"We bought this house before Odelia was born," said Marge. "And back then we were still thinking about building our own home, figuring this one would soon be too small."

"Initially we wanted two or three kids," Tex explained as he took a seat. They were out in the backyard, and he'd already raised the parasol since the sun was really turning up the heat. "But then after Odelia was born we kinda dropped the idea, didn't we?"

"We did. But we never sold the land, figuring it might bring us some money down the road. Or maybe at some point Odelia would want to build herself a home there."

"Well, it's certainly going to bring you some very good money," said Charlene as she took a nibble from her piece of toast.

"How much?" suddenly asked Dudley.

"I thought the developers had been in touch?" asked Charlene. "Didn't they make an offer?"

Tex frowned. "I think someone called me a couple of weeks ago, but I just figured it was one of them cold callers trying to sell life insurance so I hung up on them."

"We did get a letter in the mail not so long ago," said Marge. "But since we'd more or less decided to let Odelia have the land I didn't pay attention. It didn't mention a mall."

"How much did they offer?" asked Dudley eagerly.

"No price was mentioned as far as I know," said Marge. She wasn't happy that Dudley was inserting himself into the conversation, but Tex had insisted, figuring he was part of the family now. Odelia, unfortunately, had already left for work, and so had Chase, otherwise they could have weighed in, too.

"So the mall is happening?" asked Tex.

"It's still early days," said Charlene. "Which is why if you're going to sell you better do it now. Because if nothing comes of this, they'll immediately rescind their offer."

"Thanks for letting us know," said Marge, and she meant it. They could always use the extra money, now that they apparently had an extra mouth to feed in the form of Dudley.

"I think you should hold off on accepting their offer, Daddy," said the kid now. "Let them come back with a higher offer, and see how high you can get them to go before accepting." He leaned back. "I'll bet you can get them to offer you millions for that plot."

"Millions!" said Tex with a laugh. "In your dreams, buddy."

"No, I'm serious, Daddy! They need that land. Without it they can't build their precious mall. So I'll bet they're willing to pay you whatever it takes to get rid of you."

"Dudley isn't lying, Tex," said Charlene. "They seem very

willing to make you a great offer. Their exact words were: whatever it takes."

"Oh, my," said Tex, a blush of excitement mantling his cheeks. "Do you hear that, honey? We could be rich."

"Let's wait and see," said Marge, who didn't like the way Dudley kept interfering in what she considered a private family matter.

"Okay, I gotta go," said Alec, getting up. "Marge—can I have a quick word?"

She got up and followed her brother into the house. The moment they entered the kitchen he turned and said, with a frown, "What's that kid up to?"

"I don't know," she said, "but I don't trust him—do you?"

"I'm not sure." He glanced out through the window at Dudley, who was talking a mile a minute, with Tex smiling all the while. "Do you want me to check him out for you?"

"What do you mean?"

"I mean—how do you know he really is who he says he is? He could be anyone."

"I know. I was thinking the exact same thing. But Tex doesn't want to hear it. He's convinced Dudley is his son—end of discussion."

Alec nodded, and glanced around. "Got anything that belongs to Dudley?"

"Um…" She picked up a sweater the kid had dropped on one of the kitchen chairs. "You mean something like this?"

The police chief quickly extracted a few hairs and tucked them into a small plastic baggie. "And now I'm going to need something of your husband."

"DNA?" she said, understanding dawning.

"I hope he won't mind that we're going behind his back on this," said Alec as he watched Marge rifle through the laundry hamper in the laundry room off the kitchen until she found one of Tex's shirts. Alec repeated the procedure and tucked both baggies away.

"Oh, he won't be happy about it," she said. "But that can't be helped." She folded her arms across her chest. "What if he isn't Tex's son? What do we do then?"

"You let me worry about that," he said with a smile as he placed a kiss on her brow.

She gratefully put a hand on his broad chest. In moments like these she was happy that her big brother was a cop.

As soon as Alec had left, she returned to the breakfast table, where the topic under discussion was still the same as before: the millions of dollars that would be flowing into the Poole coffers now that this mall development was underway. And as Marge studied Dudley, she found herself thinking once again that she didn't trust this kid.

But how was she going to convince her husband?

Now there was an interesting problem.

24

The moment Chase had returned from walking Rambo, Odelia had swept us all into her car and rushed off. Perhaps swept is too strong a word, as it's probably hard for any human to sweep a two hundred pound dog into a car. Cajole is perhaps the better description, and so there we were, on our way to a destination unknown, four cats in the backseat, while Rambo took up space in the trunk of the car.

"Where are we going?" I asked.

"My uncle gave me a secret assignment yesterday," Odelia announced, sounding happy and excited in equal measure. "You remember Charlene's uncle who died?"

"Yeah, he fell into his own pool, right?"

"Right. Well, Uncle Alec isn't the kind of cop who likes to accept the most obvious explanation about anything, and so he wants me to look into this death a little closer. Make sure there's nothing suspicious about it."

"You think Charlene's uncle was murdered?" asked Harriet.

"I don't know. But I'm sure I'll find out."

"I like this," grunted the dog who was breathing down my neck. "Just like the old days: out on patrol, catching the bad guys."

"Did you go out on patrol a lot when you were on active duty?" asked Brutus, who, technically at least, was also a police animal, as he'd once belonged to a cop.

"Oh, yeah. All the time. Until they figured I was too old for the job, and they retired me. I'm too young to retire, so I didn't like that," he said. And then he sneezed, causing big gobs of goo to hit the back of my neck and even the back of Odelia's head.

Even if Rambo was too old to chase the bad guys, he could always hit them with his goo and make them surrender, I figured as I extracted the worst of the sticky goo from my precious blorange fur.

"Eww," Harriet whispered. "Eww, eww, eww!"

"Oh, can you have that talk now, Max?" said Odelia. "About the bowl situation, I mean?"

"What bowel situation?" said Rambo. "My bowels are just fine, in case you were wondering."

"Not the *bowel* situation—the *bowl* situation," I clarified.

"What about my bowls?" he grunted, looking annoyed.

"The thing is, Rambo," said Harriet, turning to face the large dog, "that in our household we each have our own designated bowl—two, in fact. One for water and one for kibble. And at night usually a third bowl comes out when Odelia doles out the wet food. And you can multiply that number by two, since we occupy two homes."

"Ooh, wet food," said the big dog, licking his lips with an extremely long tongue. "Rambo likes himself some wet food."

"Yes, well, so the whole point of this setup is that we only eat from our own bowl, you see? And for convenience's sake our bowls even have our names on them. So Max has his bowls, I have my bowls, Dooley has his bowls, and so does

Brutus and so do you!" She gave him a beaming smile, but the dog shook his head, causing some of his saliva to sprinkle around.

"I don't get it," he announced in that deep gravelly voice of his.

"You can only eat from the bowl that has your name on it," I said. "You can't touch any other bowl."

The dog frowned. "Oh." Then he frowned some more, causing his eyes to disappear into the folds of his face. "I see..."

"And?" said Odelia. "Do you understand the rules, Rambo? I'm sorry to have to be this strict, but with five pets in the house we need to have some house rules, you see."

"But... what if I'm hungry?" asked Rambo.

"What is he saying, Max?" asked Odelia, glancing back through the rearview mirror.

"He wants to know what he should do when he's hungry," I translated Rambo's words.

"I'll make sure to keep his bowl filled at all times," she said with a smile. "Just like I do with all you guys. Except Max, because Max has to watch his weight."

I made a face.

"Oh, don't give me that look, Maxie," said Odelia. "You know you tend to gorge."

"I don't 'gorge,'" I said stiffishly. "I simply have a very healthy appetite."

"I hear you, Max," said Rambo. "I'm exactly the same. I have the kind of appetite that makes me very cranky when I don't have anything to eat." He stared at me. "*Very* cranky."

I gulped a little. I had the distinct impression that Rambo wouldn't mind eating *me* if he ever found his bowl empty and couldn't touch my food or the others'.

"Odelia, did you stock up on dog food?" I asked, my voice a little squeaky.

"I asked Chase to pick up some more after work," she said. "I hope he doesn't forget."

"I hope so, too," grumbled Rambo, still giving me that penetrating look.

"He won't," I said in a strangled voice. "And if he does, you can always eat some of my food."

"I thought you said I can only eat from my own bowl?"

"No, but just in case of an emergency I'm sure it's fine."

"Only if you're sure, Max," said Rambo, his hooded eyes boring into mine. "Cause if not, I won't touch your bowl. I'll just find something else to eat…" And then he gave me a toothy grin, and I could see he had some very sharp incisors. Sharp and very, very big.

Gulp!

25

They'd arrived at the address Odelia's uncle had sent her. The bungalow-style house was a modest one, in a quiet neighborhood that had been built about thirty years before. It had a front yard that was well-kept, but the house itself looked a little rundown.

She set foot for the front door, four cats and one dog looking on from the sidewalk.

There was no bell to ring, but there was a sturdy brass knocker, so she used it deftly. Moments later she could hear stumbling inside, and the shuffling of feet. And when the door opened and a large man appeared, puffing from a cigarette, and only dressed in boxers and a tank top, she gave him her best smile. "Mr. Pollard? Jerry Pollard? My name is Odelia Poole, and—"

"I know who you are," he said, and stepped aside. "Come on in. Your uncle told me you were coming."

"Thanks," she said, and glanced back at her pets. She didn't think she could take them inside this time, so she gestured that they should go around the back. Who knows, maybe they could listen in on the conversation, and even save her life if Mr. Pollard turned out to be a serial killer who liked to dismember his visitors and stuff them into his freezer.

"Take a seat," he mumbled, and started dumping pizza boxes and fast food wrappers to the floor. "Don't mind the mess."

She glanced around. Apart from the obvious mess, and the telltale signs that Mr. Pollard liked to eat his dinners—and presumably his other meals, too—in front of this TV, the place was reasonably clean. She could see pictures of kids and several pictures of Jerry Pollard in better days, his arm casually slung around a woman with red hair, three red-haired grinning kids also present and accounted for.

He followed her gaze. "She lives in Florida now. Married a real estate broker. Took the kids, too."

"I'm sorry about that, Mr. Pollard," she said.

He smiled and rubbed his eyes. "So Frank Butterwick died, huh? Fell into his pool." He shook his head. "Sad affair. I liked Frank. Great guy—wonderful friend."

"You were the silent partner in his company?"

"Yeah, he needed capital to start his own business, and back then I was loaded, so I didn't mind setting him up in business for himself. He used to work for me, you know. I've been in construction my whole life, and Frank was that rare person: great at his job, and honest to a T. I was sad to see him go, but when he offered me a partnership, I jumped at the chance. Guy like that was going to make it big, I could tell. And he did. Heck, half the homes in Hampton Cove now have a pool that he installed. Or I should probably say we, though I just provided the capital and he did all the work."

"My uncle seems to think there might have been foul play involved. What do you think?"

He shrugged. "I don't know anything about that, sweetie. Frank and I didn't get in touch much. He dropped by from time to time, but from what I could see he was doing just fine —didn't need my help."

"Are you still in business, Mr. Pollard?"

"Nah—the divorce pretty much blindsided me. Took me a while to get back on my feet, and by then the business had folded. This is not a line of work you can run from behind your computer. You have to be right there, on site, all the time, keeping an eye on things. If you don't, it all goes belly-up before you know it. But I'm not complaining. Financially I'm doing okay—mostly thanks to Frank."

"So you're not aware of anyone who would have carried a grudge against him? Anyone who would want to kill him?"

Jerry Pollard hesitated for a moment, then shook his head. "Frank wasn't the kind of guy to create enemies. He was well-liked. A real people person."

"I couldn't help but notice you hesitated before answering my question, though."

He laughed. "Your uncle told me you're a pretty sharp cookie, Miss Poole. Yeah, there was one incident Frank told me about. Not that I think it matters, but…" He grimaced. "It just didn't sit well with him, you know. And I could tell it bothered him."

"What incident was that?"

"Frank started out with one guy—one builder. He pretty much took him under his wing, before hiring more people and slowly building up his company, like you do."

"And? Something happened with this builder?"

"Yeah, I guess you can say that. See, this boy didn't have any parents."

"An orphan."

Mr. Pollard nodded. "So Frank being the kind of guy he was, pretty much treated him like a son. There was a vague understanding that one day when Frank retired he'd leave the business to this kid. Which wasn't a bad offer, as the company was doing really well."

"And then what happened?"

Mr. Pollard shrugged. "I'm not sure. One day the kid simply up and left without a word. Just… walked out. Gave Frank quite a shock, I can tell you. Shook him to the core."

"Do you have a name for this person?"

"Yeah, Brett Cragg. Last I heard he lived on Grover Street, though that information dates back six months."

"When he left the company," said Odelia, nodding.

"Yup. Which just goes to show: be careful who you trust, and never, ever, hand the keys of your company to just any old fella walking in from the street."

"Do you think this Brett Cragg could be responsible for Frank's death?"

"I don't know, sweetie, but if I were you, I'd definitely talk to him."

26

"So this is what you do?" asked Rambo. "Sitting around waiting for your human?"

"Not always," I said. "Sometimes we spring into action and actually catch killers, too."

He scoffed. "Yeah, right. Looks to me like you guys have a real cushy job. Your human takes care of everything while you simply sit around and wait. In my day at the K9 unit I had to do all the work. I chased the suspects, I apprehended them, I breathed down their necks if they so much as moved a muscle."

He was certainly breathing down my neck, and I can tell you that his breath wasn't exactly like a summer breeze.

The five of us were seated in the backyard of the man Odelia had come to interview. There wasn't a lot we could do, as the back door was closed shut, and I could see no sign of any pets to talk to, so we just hunkered down for the time being, and glanced around at the world in general and the backyard in particular. It wasn't a bad backyard, as backyards go: it was about the size of a postage stamp, but what there was of it was well-maintained, with a little bit of lawn and some nice decorations in the form of a windmill and even a slide, which told me the backyard was visited by kids from time to time. There was also the obligatory grill, which would have pleased Odelia's dad to no end.

"Look, not all pets just gallivant around and are all action, action, action," said Harriet now. "Some of us use our brains before we act. Maybe you should try the same, Rambo."

I was expecting Rambo to pounce on Harriet and wait for a cop to put the cuffs on her the way he used to do when he was still an active member of the force, but much to my surprise he actually smiled, then burst into a rumbling laugh. "I like you," he said finally. "You've got spunk, little missy."

"Thanks, I guess," said Harriet doubtfully.

"So you're from the 'Think before you act' school of policing, are you? Good for you. I was always more into the 'Act first, think later' class. But then I guess I'm just built that way, whereas cats are perhaps the smarter creatures when compared to us dogs."

"Thank you, Rambo," said Harriet emphatically. She turned to us. "What have I been telling you guys all along? That cats are the brains and dogs are the brawn, right?"

I'd never even once heard Harriet say that, but before I could point this out to her, she was already moving on.

"I think we would make a great team, Rambo," she said. "You're the muscle and I'm the finesse. So maybe you should join us."

"Us? What's this us you're talking about?"

"We're the proud members of Odelia's posse," said Harriet. "She's an amateur sleuth, you see, and we're her secret weapon. Like… she's Charlie and we're her angels?"

"So you solve crime, huh? Catch killers and such?"

"That's right," said Harriet, tilting her head proudly. "You're looking at Hampton Cove's premier feline crime fighters."

"So if you're so good at what you do, then why do you need a guard dog is what I'm wondering."

"Um…"

I smiled, for Rambo had performed the ultimate feat: he'd managed to shut Harriet up. I'd never managed this myself, so it was with a certain measure of admiration that I regarded the big old dog now.

"Look, this killer took us by surprise, all right?" said Harriet, never one to be stumped for long. "The last thing you suspect is for a cat killer to show up in your own home, and grab you before you know what's happening."

"You have to remain vigilant, Harriet," said Rambo, speaking like one who knows. "If there's one thing I've learned from all my years on the force it's that you can never let your guard down, no matter what."

"Do you ever let your guard down?" I asked.

"Me? Never! I mean, you probably think I'm some lumbering, drooling, smelly has-been, right?"

"Oh, no," I said, though that was exactly what I'd been thinking.

"Wrong! I'm always alert. Always looking, always listening," he said, as his eyes swiveled this way and that. "That's why I'm so good at what I do. You never see me coming."

I could definitely smell him coming, though.

"The bad guys underestimate me, and that's my secret weapon. They laugh at me—oh, look at that stupid mutt. Ha ha ha. And BOOM! I pounce and that's the end of them."

"Good for you," I said without much conviction. Talk is cheap, after all, and this big dog could most certainly talk.

He suddenly cut his eyes to me, and said, "I see a lot of me in you, Max."

"Oh?" I said, surprised.

"Yeah, you're also fat, out of shape, ugly… a mouth-breather. But underneath all that flab and blubber beats the heart of a true warrior."

I didn't know whether to be pleased or annoyed. It's always tough when they wrap the compliments in a thick layer of insults. "Um, thanks, I guess," I said.

"Or you, Dooley. You look like a weakling. A dumbass. But you're a lot smarter than you look, am I right?"

"I… think so?" said Dooley uncertainly.

"Or look at Brutus. Underneath all that bluster and posturing lurks a sly dog. And then there's Harriet, of course. She may look like a drama queen, a prissy princess, a giggle-puss, but she's smart as a whip, aren't you?"

"Uh-huh?" said Harriet with a frown.

"So yeah, I guess we make a great team, just like you said," he said with a yawn, then placed his head on his front paws and closed his eyes. And soon he was snoring away again, making the air tremble with the volume of his snores.

"Do you think he's asleep, Max?" asked Dooley.

"I think there's a good chance of that, Dooley," I said.

"But he said he's always vigilant, always alert—sees all, hears all, knows all…"

I waved a hand in front of the dog's closed eyes, then poked him in the squishy nose.

"Nope," I said. "He's definitely fast asle—"

"Gotcha!" suddenly roared Rambo, and placed his big paw on top of my head!

"Aaargh!" I screamed, much surprised.

And then he burst into a booming laugh, and soon Harriet, Brutus and Dooley were all laughing along.

"The look on your face, Max!" Harriet squealed. "Priceless!"

"Yeah, you should have seen yourself, Max!" said Brutus. "You looked absolutely terrified!"

"He is always alert, Max!" said Dooley. "Amazing, Mr. Rambo."

"Thanks, Dooley. Just a small demonstration of my secret power. And now I'm going to take a nap for real. If this cat killer shows his ugly face, wake me up, all right?"

And then he went right back to snoring like a lumberjack. And this time I wasn't going anywhere near him. Once bitten and all that.

And when half an hour later Odelia rounded the bungalow to fetch us, we were still sitting motionless, while our guard dog was sleeping the sleep of the dead.

So much for unwavering vigilance…

27

When Odelia saw her four cats, guarded by a dog that was fast asleep, the sight didn't do much to quell her fears for their safety. She'd known that her uncle wouldn't be able to supply her with the best dog the K9 unit had to offer, but this Rambo wasn't exactly what she'd had in mind when she'd asked for a guard dog.

Then again, she couldn't very well ask Chase to keep an eye on them all the time. So it was imperative that whoever had attacked them at home was found and found fast.

So when she was back in her car, and had buckled her seatbelt, she called her uncle.

"Hey, Uncle Alec," she said. "I was just calling in for an update on this cat killer?"

"Nothing new, honey," said her uncle. "I have some of my people asking around, but whoever this guy was, he was careful not to be seen entering or leaving the house."

"Okay… So maybe fingerprints? Anything?"

"Nothing so far. Why? Aren't your cats happy with their new friend?"

"Not exactly," she said, though she didn't want to say

more, for Rambo was in the back of the car, and he definitely wasn't sleeping now.

"Don't let his appearance deceive you," said her uncle. "He's one of the best we've got. Or at least he used to be when he was a full-fledged member of the team. He may be retired now, but I'm sure he's still got that killer instinct you want to see in a guard dog."

She glanced back, and saw that Rambo had placed his voluminous head on the top of the backseat, slobbering all over the upholstery. He was certainly killing her car.

"So did you get anything from this guy Jerry Pollard?"

"Maybe." And she told her uncle about the builder who'd run away.

"Interesting," he said. "Maybe I'll run it by Charlene. She might remember something. She and her uncle had a good connection."

"I'll try to find out where he lives, and see if I can't track him down," she said.

"You do that, honey. Um…"

"What is it?"

"I'm running a check on Dudley. I took a strand of his hair and one from your dad."

"You want to see if he's really Dad's son."

"Yup. According to Marge your dad is really taken in with the kid. She's not so sure, though."

"He seems nice enough."

"Yeah, I know, but I guess Marge feels it pays to be careful. After all, what do we know about him? Nothing."

"No, sure. But I think the DNA test will come back a positive match. He even looks like Dad—minus the ears."

"Yeah, well, I'm of the same opinion as my sister. You can never be too careful these days. Oh, and did you know about the plot of land your mom and dad own and that now may be worth a great deal of money?"

"What?"

"Ask your mom. She'll tell you all about it." And with a light chuckle, he disconnected.

"Plot of land?" she said, staring before her.

"What's going on?" asked Max.

"It looks like my parents are going to be rich," she said. "And my uncle is running a DNA test on Dudley, to see if he really is who he says he is."

"Very prudent," growled Rambo. "You can't trust anyone these days. The world is full of cheaters and swindlers and thieves and con artists. Not to mention murderers, backstabbers and other scum of the earth."

And on that cheerful note, he put down his head again.

Odelia started the engine and drove off, in search of this mysterious young man who'd joined then left Frank Butterwick's company.

It didn't take her long to find out where he lived: she simply asked around in the neighborhood Jerry Pollard had indicated. When she showed up on his doorstep, though, he didn't answer the bell, and when she knocked on the door, no one came.

His next-door-neighbor, who was pruning her hedge, saw her peeking in through the window, and announced, "That won't do you any good, honey. He moved out last month."

"Where to?" she asked.

But the woman shrugged. "He didn't tell me and I didn't ask." And continued her pruning.

"Great," Odelia muttered. And as she walked back to her car, her phone dinged, and when she looked she saw she'd received a message from her mom. It contained a link, and when she clicked on the link, it took her to a Gofundme page, set up by… Vesta Muffin!

"Oh, dear," she murmured. As she got back into her car,

she showed the cats the page. "Looks like Gran is collecting money for a new car," she announced.

"Nice," said Brutus. "I like the look of that Escalade."

"Yeah, I like it, too," she said. "But the way Gran drives I pity the people who get in her way."

In fact it probably wouldn't be a bad idea to get Gran to take her driving test again. But that probably wasn't in the cards.

"Why don't *you* get a new car?" asked Harriet. "You could set up one of these Gofundme pages, too, and get rid of this piece of junk."

She smiled. "It may be a piece of junk, Harriet, but I'm attached to my car."

Her clunky but precious pickup was the first car she'd ever bought, with money she'd earned herself, and she didn't want to get rid of it until she had to.

"As long as it keeps on rolling, I will keep on driving it," she announced, and as she said the words, suddenly there was a loud crunching sound, and the engine... died!

28

Harriet wasn't feeling particularly happy. This was not an unusual state of affairs for the gorgeous white Persian, but this time she could attribute her unhappiness to a very specific incident: her boyfriend admitting that he had a habit of peeing in her bowl. The fact that he also liked to pee in Max and Dooley's bowls didn't much interest her, but he shouldn't have peed in hers—that was obvious.

So she was upset, and when she was upset she liked to make it known to everyone around her, and most specifically to the person she was upset with, in this case Brutus.

Problem was that this cat killer was still around, and now Odelia had more or less corralled them all together with either Chase as their protector, or Rambo. So she couldn't even walk off on a huff and ignore Brutus the way he should be ignored after what he'd put her through. She was forced to stick together with the offender, and act as if nothing happened, which was agony for a cat as proficient at expressing her anger as she was.

Lucky for her she was also a very clever kitten, so the moment Odelia had called Triple-A and was patiently waiting for the tow truck to show up, she sidled up to her human and said, ever so sweetly, "I had a great idea, Odelia, and I wanted to run it by you if you've got a moment."

"Oh, sure, Harriet," said Odelia. "What's on your mind?"

"Well, you know how Rambo and Chase are supposed to protect us?"

"Uh-huh?"

"The thing is, I'm pretty sure that cat killer was in fact targeting me, not the others. So I think it only stands to reason that Chase and Rambo should protect me, and let the others go about their business the way they usually do." She gave Odelia a mournful look. "You know the burden us females have to carry, always being targeted by some nasty element of the male species? Max, Dooley and Brutus simply don't have that kind of experience, nor do I feel they should be punished because I'm the one under attack."

"You think the attacker was gunning for you, is that what you're saying?"

"Absolutely. And isn't that always the case? So if you could ask Chase to guard my back from now on, and Rambo, too, I'd be very much obliged, Odelia, sweetie."

Odelia, who wasn't in the best of moods, after her car had broken down, eyed her a little strangely, Harriet thought. "You and Brutus have been fighting again, haven't you?"

"Just one of those lovers' tiffs," said Harriet airily. "You know how it goes. I'll bet you and Chase go through that sort of thing all the time."

"No, actually we don't," said Odelia. "So what have you been fighting about this time?"

She sighed. "I really don't want to bother you with my petty problems, Odelia. You have so much on your mind already."

"Indulge me," said Odelia.

"Well…" She glanced over to where Brutus stood chatting

with Max and Dooley and Rambo, and frowned. "Brutus confessed that sometimes he pees in our bowls. Not a full tinkle, you see, but just a pre-pee or pre-tinkle, as he calls it, when he feels he won't be able to reach his litter box in time. So he unleashes a few drops into the first bowl he sees, which just so happens to be either mine or Dooley's or Max's and not his own if you please, and then he proceeds to his box for the main course, as it were. And when I asked him why he doesn't pee in his own bowl, he didn't really have an answer for me."

Odelia smiled, which struck Harriet as highly inappropriate indeed. "Maybe I should ask Mom to put a small plastic tub in the bedroom, just for these kinds of midnight emergencies," she said. "In the old days people actually put a chamber pot in their bedrooms, so maybe we should dust off that old custom for you guys."

"Oh, *I* don't have a problem reaching my litter box in time," Harriet assured her human. "It's only Brutus who seems to have an acute bladder control issue."

"Harriet, honey, you can't really blame Brutus because he has a small bladder. I mean, I agree he shouldn't have done it, but I think we can all agree that he didn't do it on purpose. It was just an accident."

"An accident is when it happens once," Harriet argued, starting to wonder in whose corner Odelia was: hers or Brutus's. "But this happened several times—six times, to be exact. And six times doesn't qualify as an accident but more as something he's been doing on purpose, just because he can."

"I'm sure Brutus was simply too embarrassed to talk about his midnight mishaps. It is a little embarrassing for a proud cat like him to have to admit that he can't hold up his pee. And so instead of being angry with him, I think you should have some compassion."

"Compassion?" asked Harriet, as if the word was new to her. "What do you mean?"

"I mean that this isn't something Brutus can do much about. It happens to humans, too, you know. When we get older, sometimes we simply lose the ability to control our bladders. And sometimes it leads to these little mishaps." She patted Harriet's head. "Just be gentle with Brutus, sweetheart. He's a good cat, and you should be proud to call him your boyfriend."

"Mh," said Harriet, not convinced. "So what are you saying? That you won't assign Chase and Rambo as my private bodyguards from now on?"

"I'm sure you weren't the only target," said Odelia, adding insult to injury with these words. "If you were, he wouldn't have put you all in that chest and set it on fire, would he?"

She hated this kind of spurious argument, so she gave Odelia an unhappy look and turned away. She'd specifically asked Odelia because she figured women had to stick together in a man's world, and all Odelia had for her were empty words like 'compassion' and 'mishaps' and vague promises about 'chamber pots,' whatever that was.

Fat lot of good that did her, she meant to say. And when she joined the others again, she vowed to find a different solution to her problem—one that didn't involve that treacherous Odelia Poole.

What good was it to have a human if she wasn't in your corner when it mattered?

29

"Bellamy Butt Movers and Shakers? Yes, this is Odelia Poole. I'm a reporter for the Hampton Cove Gazette, and I'm working on a story about the death of Frank Butterwick. Mr. Butterwick had someone who worked for him that I'd like to speak to. And it is my understanding that you helped move him out of his apartment a couple of months ago."

She gave the person on the other end of the line the name and address of Brett Cragg, and was gratified to hear that Bellamy Butt's aptly named moving company had, indeed, moved Mr. Cragg out of his apartment. What she wasn't happy about was that the address they'd moved him to was located in the great state of Ohio. They did have a phone number on record for the young builder, and she gratefully jotted it down.

Her next call told her that the number had been disconnected, though, which made her investigations into Charlene's uncle hit another snag. And as she patiently waited for the tow truck to pick up her pickup, she wondered about her next course of action.

So she'd talked to Frank Butterwick's former associate, the police had already talked to his current workers, and she'd tried to hunt down his very first worker and failed.

Where did that leave her? Exactly nowhere.

And she was just wondering where to go from here when the tow truck finally arrived and for the next ten minutes she watched as her pickup was being hauled away.

She'd already called her grandmother and asked her for a ride, and when the old lady drove up in Odelia's mom's ancient Peugeot, she was glad to finally be mobile again.

"You should do like me," said Gran as she steered the vehicle in the direction of town. "You should start one of them Gofungus things. You'll have a new car in no time."

"I don't think Gofundme is designed to help people buy themselves a new car, Gran," she said. "Besides, I'm sure my pickup will be fixed soon."

"That old thing? I'd take it to the junkyard if I were you."

"The guy who came to pick it up said it was probably a faulty fuel pump. I'll have the car back tomorrow already." He'd also said she was extremely lucky that she didn't end up rolling her stalled pickup straight into oncoming traffic and getting herself killed in a head-on collision, but she wisely kept that bit of information to herself.

"Better get yourself a new set of wheels is what I say. That wreck you call a car is going to cost you an arm and a leg in repairs over the next couple of years."

"Well, I happen to like that old wreck, and as long as I can keep driving it, I will."

"You know what? As soon as these Gofunky people have collected enough money so I can buy myself that Escalade, you can have this car. How about that?" She tapped the wheel. "It's still a pretty decent old thing. Pretty sure you'll be able to get a couple thousand more miles out of it."

"Thanks, but I'm sure Mom will be glad to have her car back."

"Marge doesn't need a car," grunted Gran. "Besides, she'll be a millionaire soon. She'll be able to buy herself all the cars she needs."

"Oh, that's right. I didn't even know Mom and Dad owned that land."

"Nobody knew! I think they completely forgot about it themselves, the doofuses."

"So you think they'll sell?"

"Of course they'll sell! They'd be crazy not to! Now I know that Marge has an eccentric streak, and your father isn't exactly the sharpest tool in God's big shed, but even they wouldn't be so dumb as to leave a couple million dollars on the table."

"Millions? You really think they'll fetch millions for that piece of land?"

"From what Charlene said this morning? It sure looks like it to me."

"Yeah, I suppose a deal like that is too good to turn down."

"Which is exactly what I told them. And they should move fast, too. These developer types are tricky. They'll pay you millions today and pennies on the dollar tomorrow—for the same land!"

"Do you think that mall will actually be built?"

"Of course that mall will be built. Everybody wants money, honey. And politicians like Charlene most of all. I'm pretty sure she'll be getting all kinds of kickbacks and backhanders, and so will the other council members." She tapped her nose. "Take it from me—a lot of people will get filthy rich off this deal, and Hampton Cove will be left with a town center that's deader than a dodo. But hey, that's progress for you: some people get rich, and others get poor. Let's just make sure we're on the right side of the equation."

"If you really believe this mall will turn downtown Hampton Cove into a dead zone, don't you think we should organize some kind of protest? Try to convince Charlene to stop this development?"

Gran shrugged as she sat hunched over the steering wheel, driving through town at breakneck speed as was her habit. "Fat lot of good that'll do. These two-faced politicians will do whatever they want to do. They're not going to listen to the likes of you or me."

"Why not? Your son is Charlene's boyfriend, which practically makes her your daughter-in-law."

Gran grinned. "Where have you been, honey? Nobody ever listens to me! And the ones who are least likely to do what I say is my own damn family!"

Odelia smiled. Gran had a point. "I still think that if you hate that mall, you should tell Charlene. You never know—maybe she'll actually listen."

"Yeah, right," muttered Gran, and aggressively bypassed a vehicle, gesticulating widely as she did, then took a hard right and pulled over, stomping on the brakes.

Odelia was propelled forward, saved by her seatbelt, and so were the cats. Who wasn't so lucky was Rambo, who'd been seated in the trunk of the car, due to his sheer size, and now came rocketing forward and plopped down on top of the cats, burying them in a mountain of dog.

By the time he'd managed to scramble out of the car, four cats were gasping for air, and looking more than a little unhappy.

"When you said you'd hire a guard dog to keep us safe, you didn't mention that he'd try to kill us!" said Harriet, who was never shy to voice her grievances loud and clear.

"I'm sorry," said Gran. "Things will get better once Gofunkus buys me my Escalade."

"Or a whole lot worse," murmured Max.

They all stood on the sidewalk and watched Gran take off again—like a bat out of hell.

"She should really learn how to drive," said Brutus.

"Yeah, for the leader of the neighborhood watch she's this neighborhood's biggest threat," said Max. "In fact we probably need a second watch to watch the first watch."

"I'm never setting foot in a car with Gran again," Harriet vowed.

"I think she means well," said Dooley.

"I'm hungry," said Rambo with a yawn. "When do we eat?"

"Step into my office," Odelia said. "As long as this cat killer is on the loose, I think it's best if you guys stick close to me."

It was with some reluctance that her cats followed her into her office. Then again, she couldn't very well ask Chase to keep an eye on them again after last night's eventful shift. And even though they now had their own watchdog in the form of Rambo, she still felt more relaxed when the entire cat troupe stayed where she could see them at all times.

And so once again she was faced with her initial conundrum.

How to proceed with the Frank Butterwick case!

30

Gran arrived home in record time and parked her car haphazardly at the curb, then hurried into the house. She'd left her phone in her room that morning and she felt bereft without the little technological wonder.

For one thing, she wanted to know where they stood with the Goflunky campaign. How many thousands of dollars they'd already collected and when she could finally go and buy herself that shiny new Escalade!

She'd already visited the car dealership that morning and had picked out the make and model. Now all she needed was the cash to buy the darn thing and they were in business.

She stormed into her bedroom, picked her phone from the nightstand and then stormed down again. Only she must have missed a step, for suddenly she faltered and before she knew what was happening she was airborne… for just a couple of seconds, unfortunately, and then she was tumbling down the steps—face forward!

She hit the stairs hard, and skidded down the last few

steps, and when finally she came to a full stop, she was still holding onto her phone, wondering what in the name of all that was holy had happened!

"Gran!" said Dudley, who was the first to arrive on the crash scene. "Are you all right?"

"First off, I'm not your grandmother," she grunted. "And what are you doing there gawking at me like a dead fish? Help me up, will you?"

"Are you hurt?" asked Dudley, sounding surprised that she was still talking after taking such a tumble.

"Of course I'm not hurt," she said annoyedly. "Takes more than an awkward landing to put a dent in this old gal." She still checked herself for broken bones or sprains or other calamities, but the only thing that hurt was her pride. "Lucky escape," she muttered as she slapped Dudley's eager ministrations away.

She glanced back, wondering why she'd taken that sudden tumble. And then she saw it: the carpet runner had come loose somewhere halfway up the stairs. She gave it a closer look, and saw that the screws holding the darn thing in place had come unstuck.

"Weirdest thing," she said as she vowed to give her son-in-law a piece of her mind.

"I better get that fixed," said Dudley as he saw what she was looking at.

"Wasn't like that this morning," said Vesta. "Pretty sure it was fine then."

"These screws can be fiddly," said the kid. "Especially if the runner was screwed down a long time ago."

"I'll tell Tex to fix it."

"Nah, don't bother," said Dudley. "I'll do it."

"Thanks," she said grudgingly. She had to admit that the kid was all right. Not only had he been more than helpful just now, but it was obvious he wasn't one of them lazy kids who liked to lie around on the couch all day, playing with their stupid Playstation.

"You're welcome," said Dudley with a big smile.

"Well, I gotta get going," she announced, and was out the door in a flash. And as she walked back to her car, a sudden ache in her shoulder gave her pause. "Ouch!" she said, as she rubbed the sore spot. So maybe her little accident *had* put a dent in her.

🐾

Tex had been working nonstop all morning, seeing one patient after another. Some days were like that: the whole town population suddenly seemed to have fallen ill. And on other days it was so quiet he practically didn't see a single patient all day.

So he was glad when suddenly Vesta came sticking her head in the door.

"Am I glad to see you!" he said. "It's been crazy all morning!"

"I'm not here to work," she announced. "I'm here because I just fell down the stairs and now my shoulder hurts."

He probably should have uttered a few words of concern that the aged mother of his wife had suffered a serious accident, but instead he inwardly cursed a receptionist who never came into work, and even when she did it was only to add to his workload instead.

"Take a seat," he said curtly, as he'd just said goodbye to Ida Baumgartner and Blanche Captor had only just gotten up from her chair in the waiting room but now sat down again with a few muttered curses under her breath when she heard Vesta's words.

"So what happened?" he asked once Vesta had closed the door and taken a seat.

"Are you deaf? I just told you. I fell down the stairs and now my shoulder hurts."

"What stairs? The ones at home?"

"Yeah—the runner's come unstuck. Loose screw. The kid will fix it," she added.

"Dudley was there when it happened?"

"Yeah. Must have heard me take a tumble and helped me up. Very sweet of him," she added, a little begrudgingly.

"Oh, he's a very sweet kid," Tex agreed. "I'm very lucky with a son like that."

"Yeah, yeah. Now are you going to take a look at my shoulder or are you going to keep flapping your gums about this so-called son of yours?"

Tex walked around his desk and invited his mother-in-law to take a seat on a little stool, then made her take off her tracksuit vest and carefully inspected the bruise on her shoulder.

"Why 'so-called son?'" he asked. "Don't you think Dudley is mine?"

"I don't know, Tex," she said. "And I'm sure once Alec runs that DNA test we'll know more. But until we do, I'm not taking Dudley's word for it."

He frowned. "DNA test? What DNA test?"

"The one Marge asked Alec to run. So how is it? Am I going to live or what?"

"It's just a bruise," he said. "Nothing to worry about." He was shocked to hear his wife and brother-in-law hadn't told him about this DNA test—going behind his back like that.

"It's this tracksuit," said Vesta proudly. "Scarlett is always making fun of me that I like to wear these tracksuits but if she'd taken that tumble she probably wouldn't have survived.

Now are you going to give me something for the bruise? I haven't got all day."

So Tex prescribed his mother-in-law a cream to put on that bruise, but even as he was typing out the prescription, dark thoughts gathered in his mind—such as it was.

31

Being locked up inside an office with one cat who seemed annoyed to be in our presence (Harriet), one cat who was anxious to get home and be near his litter box (Brutus) and one dog who had been doing nothing but eat since we got there (Rambo) isn't exactly my idea of a good time.

And we had this mysterious cat killer to thank for it. He might not have taken our lives, but he'd certainly taken our freedom now that Odelia had decided we should stick close to either her or another member of her family until this attacker was caught.

Odelia had arranged for a large helping of dog kibble to be delivered to her office, and a (slightly less large) helping of cat kibble, and for once we all got to share one big bowl of water, but apart from that, the situation was less than ideal.

"I'd take you home but I have to finish this story," she said when I gave her a troubled look.

She'd opened the back door, which led out onto a sort of small courtyard where we could do our business if we needed to, in the tiny patch of greenery, and amongst Dan

Goory's roses, of which he was particularly proud, but that was pretty much it.

"Here," she said when I continued to give her less-than-happy glances, and handed me a tablet computer. "Make yourselves useful and try to figure out where I can find Charlene's uncle's former associate, will you? His name is Brett Cragg."

So we gathered around the tablet computer, Brutus, Dooley and I, and started idly surfing the web, in search of a clue as to where we could find this Brett Cragg person.

He wasn't on Facebook, though, and not on LinkedIn either, or Twitter or Instagram. In fact we didn't find a trace of him anywhere, which made me think he was one of those rare individuals who didn't spend their every waking hour poring over social media.

"Max?" whispered Brutus, darting a surreptitious eye at Odelia. "Maybe we can escape!"

"Escape?" I said. "Why do you want to escape? We're safe in here. No one can get at us as long as we stay close to Odelia and Rambo." Trading one's safety for one's freedom is a tough bargain, but one I'd grudgingly embraced. Not so, apparently, my friend.

"But we talked about this, Max," he said. "We were going to recruit Clarice. She can be the one protecting us from now on. And I think she'll probably do a better job than Rambo."

We both cast a quick glance at the big dog, who was now snoring loudly, drool bubbling on his lips and dripping onto Odelia's nice office carpet. He'd already eaten half a bag of dog kibble, and I had the distinct impression that second half wouldn't last much longer either.

"All he does is sleep and eat," said Brutus, and not unreasonably either. "I don't think he's cut out to be a guard dog."

"No, he doesn't seem to be the guard dog Odelia had envisioned when she hired him," I agreed.

"So why don't we slip out the back now, and see if we can't find Clarice?!"

Dooley didn't seem overly excited by the prospect of this 'great escape' either.

"But what is Odelia going to say? She'll be very upset with us if we run away."

"Odelia will understand," said Brutus. "If we explain to her why we did it, she'll be okay."

"And what about Harriet?" asked Dooley.

We all looked over to where Harriet was lying on a settee, idly licking her fur and pretending the rest of us didn't exist.

"Harriet is still very upset with me," said Brutus sadly. "So I don't think she'll exactly sound the alarm if we make a break for it now."

"And what if Clarice says no?" I asked. "Then what do we do?"

"Then we come back here—chances are Odelia won't even notice we're gone."

This time three pairs of cat's eyes swiveled to our human, who was typing away at her desk, her focus on her story unwavering.

Brutus was right. Odelia probably wouldn't notice if we took off for a little while.

"All right," I finally said. "So let's go and find Clarice."

"I would feel a lot safer with Clarice in our corner," Dooley said, trying to convince himself to go along with Brutus's daring scheme.

"Of course you would!" said Brutus. "This cat killer is no match for Clarice. So let's go already, before Rambo wakes up and alerts Odelia."

And so our adventure began. Ever so quietly we snuck out of the office, down the corridor, then out into the miniature courtyard and then it was a cinch for us to scale the wall that surrounded Dan's little patch of green and we were out.

"I hope she's not out in the woods," I said.

Clarice doesn't have a fixed abode, like the rest of us do. She can usually be found searching the dumpsters behind the stores on Main Street, but she's just as likely to hang out in the woods in the hilly area near our town, where Hetta Fried owns the Writer's Lodge, a cabin she likes to rent out to writers and artists. And since said artists and writers are rich enough to be able to afford Hetta's cabin in the woods, they're usually not too stingy to share their copious meals with Clarice.

We quickly crossed the street and then we were traipsing along the sidewalk.

"See?" said Brutus. "This is perfectly safe. Even if this cat killer were still stalking us, which I think is unlikely, he would never abduct us in broad daylight, in front of all these people. There's safety in numbers, fellas, and so we've got nothing to worry about!"

I still wasn't exactly at ease, in spite of those numbers Brutus found so safe. It only took one maniac to snatch us from the street and deposit us in the back of his van and that would be it. Game over for us!

So when finally we reached the back alley that Clarice considers her own private property, I breathed a sigh of intense relief.

"Clarice?" I called out when we entered the alley. "Are you there?"

The dumpsters were full to the bursting point, as the town's sanitation services had yet to pick them up, so there was every chance Clarice was around.

"Clarice!" Brutus called out. "We need to talk to you!"

"I don't think she's here," said Dooley as we reached the end of the alley and still there was no sign of our feral friend.

"She could be out by the strip mall," Brutus said. In lieu of an actual mall we have a modest strip of shops with a parking lot attached to it located on the road that leads into Hampton Cove. Shops that will probably all disappear when the big mall opens its doors.

"What are you yelling about?" suddenly a cranky voice sounded from underneath the dumpster closest to me.

"Clarice!" I said. "Am I glad to see you!"

"I'd love to say the same thing, but I'm not happy to see you," she said, and yawned. "I was just having a nice nap, until you came along, with all your screaming and shouting. What do you want?"

"We have a proposition for you, Clarice," said Brutus, plastering a wide smile onto his face.

"If you're asking me to marry you, you can forget about it. I'm not the marrying type."

"No, I don't want to marry you!" said Brutus quickly.

She cocked her head and gave him a sly look. "Why? I'm not good enough for you? Is that it?"

"No, of course not!"

"Then what's the problem? I'm too outspoken? Too loud? Too fond of my freedom?"

Brutus gave me a helpless look, and so I took over from him.

"We've been attacked," I announced. "A madman shoved us into a sort of trunk or chest and set fire to us. It was only through sheer luck that we escaped with our lives."

"That doesn't sound good," said Clarice, and casually licked a very sharp-looking claw. "But at the risk of sounding callous, what does that have to do with me?"

"Well, since the incident Odelia has tasked her boyfriend with our protection, and she's also hired a retired police dog. Neither solution really sits well with us. Chase because he obviously hates the job of babysitting a brace of cats, and because he has his day job to think about, and the dog because, well, he doesn't really seem to care."

"So we thought of you, Clarice," said Brutus fervently.

"That's very nice of you, Brutus," she said sweetly. "I always like it when cats think of me. Now just spit it out already, Max. What do you want?"

"We want you to watch over us. To be our bodyguard. To make sure this cat killer doesn't come near us again."

For a moment, Clarice simply stared at me, then she burst into a loud side-splitting laugh. "Me!" she cried. "Guard you lot!"

"Yes, that's the general idea," I said.

"She's not going to do it," said Dooley, shaking his head. "She thinks the idea is stupid."

"Well, it is a stupid idea, Dooley," said Clarice, wiping the tears from her eyes. "I'm not a guard cat—I can look after myself, sure. But to look after a couple of jelly-belly lily-livered pampered house cats like you guys? I'd have to be crazy to take the job!"

"For your information we're not entirely pampered," I said stiffly. "In fact I'd say we can take pretty good care of ourselves most of the time. But this cat killer—he just came out of nowhere. Took us by surprise."

"And it wasn't a nice surprise," Dooley pointed out.

"And so another pair of eyes wouldn't be a luxury."

"Clarice, please help us," said Dooley. "You're the only one we can trust. And the only cat who's so… so… so tough!"

Her smirk died away as she regarded Dooley. "Oh, Dooley, Dooley," she said. "That's very nice of you to say, honey, but I'm just not cut out for this kind of job. I've only ever had to take care of myself—and if I take on the responsibility of you guys and something happens to you, I'd never forgive myself."

"I'm sure nothing is going to happen," I said. "This cat killer—we haven't seen a sign of him since it happened. But just to be on the safe side…"

"Yeah, just as a precaution, see," said Brutus.

"I don't want to die, Clarice," said Dooley, directing a pleading look at the tough street cat. "I'm too young to die, and so are my friends. Won't you please help us—please?"

She gave him a little smile, then finally screwed up her face. "Aah! I'm so going to regret this! Okay—fine! I'll take the job! But if you go and die on me, I swear I'll kill you!"

32

Odelia had been working steadily, typing up her article about the attack on her cats, then an article about the mall development plans, and an article about her dad finding his son after all these years. And when finally she leaned back and stretched, she glanced around and was surprised to find that instead of four cats and one dog, suddenly she was in the presence of *five* cats and one dog.

"Clarice?" she said, blinking as she regarded the scrawny cat, who looked as if she'd been run over by a car. "What are you doing here?"

"Your cats hired me as their bodyguard," Clarice growled. "What can I say? It's hard to say no to Dooley."

"I convinced her," said Dooley, beaming.

"Yeah, yeah, yeah," said Clarice. "Don't rub it in. So what's the plan?" she asked. "And what can you tell me about this so-called cat killer?"

"Nothing so-called about it," said Brutus. "That guy did try to kill us."

"He hasn't killed you yet, has he? So he's not a cat killer but a wannabe killer."

"The plan is for my cats not to leave the house if they don't have to, and if they do, always to be accompanied by either Rambo or Chase, who's their official bodyguard."

"Well, so now I'm their official bodyguard, so Chase is off the hook, and so is fatso over there," she added with a gesture of the head in the direction of the sleeping dog.

"Are you sure you can handle this threat?" asked Odelia. She admired Clarice for her survival instinct and the gumption with which she went through life, but didn't think she was a match against her cats' attacker.

"Oh, don't you worry about me, toots," said Clarice. "It's the would-be killer you should feel sorry for." And to show Odelia she meant business, she unsheathed a particularly sharp-looking long claw.

Odelia had to gulp at the sight of it. "All right," she said. "So I'll tell Chase he's relieved of his duties. I am still going to ask you to never go anywhere without Rambo. My uncle vouches for him. Says he's the best of the best, and I'd feel much easier in my mind knowing he's keeping an eye on you."

"All right," said Clarice after a particularly scathing glance at the big dog. "We'll let him tag along. For now."

"Have you discovered anything new about this cat killer?" asked Max.

"Not yet," she said. "And my uncle tells me he has no clue as to his identity or what he was doing in Mom and Dad's house either."

"Too bad," said Max.

"So whatever you do, and wherever you go—please be careful, you guys, all right?"

She watched her cats walk out of the office with mixed emotions. She didn't want to see them harmed, but she didn't want to keep them locked inside all the time either—something they clearly hated.

But then Clarice turned and gave her a wink. "I'll take good care of your babies, honey. Don't you worry about a thing."

"Me, too," said Rambo with a yawn, and waddled off.

※

Marge had arrived home from work early, and decided to make herself a nice cup of tea before she got started on the backyard. The back part of the garden had become an eyesore, with roses that needed deadheading, and weeds that needed pulling.

Usually her mom took care of that kind of stuff, or even her husband, but lately both had been too busy to bother, and Marge didn't mind a bit of gardening from time to time.

She didn't exactly possess a green thumb, but she wasn't certain death to plants either.

And she'd just popped a capsule into her coffee maker and poured water into the reservoir when suddenly she got the shock of a lifetime—literally! It was as if she'd touched a live wire, and her teeth clattered and she thought she smelled burnt rubber.

Moments later she was on the floor, and wondering what had happened. And when Dudley came running into the kitchen, exclaiming, "Marge! What happened—oh, my God!" she realized she'd been in one of those household accidents you always read so much about. The kind that allegedly, and according to insurance company statistics, kill no less than 120.000 people per annum in the United States alone.

"I-I think I electrocuted myself," she said as she got up off the floor with Dudley's assistance.

"Your hair!" he said, glancing up at her do.

She touched her hands to her hair, and it was indeed feeling a little frizzier than usual.

"How did this happen?" she asked, still feeling a little dizzy.

"I don't know," said Dudley. "I heard what sounded like a loud popping sound, and when I came running in I saw smoke coming out of the coffee maker—and your hair!"

Together they inspected the coffee maker, and indeed: it was completely fried.

"Must be faulty wiring," said Dudley as he took a towel and pulled the plug from the wall socket. He held up the wire: it was blackened, the plastic having melted away. "You're lucky to be alive, Marge," he said earnestly. "Electrocution is no joke."

"No, I don't think it's very funny," she murmured as she staggered a bit, until Dudley helpfully led her to a chair and gently set her down.

"Oh, dear, oh, dear, oh, dear," said the young man. "This is the second accident in one day. First Grandma Muffin and now you."

"My mom?" she asked, alarmed. "What happened to my mom?"

"Didn't she tell you? She fell down the stairs. She's all right," he quickly added when Marge made to get up. "She's one tough old bird, that one."

"She is very tough," Marge agreed, but still didn't like to hear she'd taken a tumble. Even tough old birds could break their necks falling down the stairs. "How did it happen?"

"The runner came unstuck," said Dudley. "I already screwed it back in place again, don't worry. This thing, though," he added, glancing at the coffee maker, "is a total loss I'm afraid."

"Thanks, Dudley," she said, bringing a distraught hand to her head.

"That's all right," said Dudley. "I mean, I know you're not particularly fond of me and all, and I totally understand that," he hastened to add when she opened her mouth to protest. "To discover that your husband fathered a son once upon a time—that would be a hard pill to swallow for anyone. And I wanted to tell you that if you really don't want me to be here—or to be part of your husband's life—I'll be gone, Marge. Absolutely."

She studied the young man for a moment. He seemed genuinely concerned about her, and serious when he spoke these words. So she nodded. "You can stay," she said. "For now," she added when a big smile appeared on his face.

"Thanks, Marge," he said. "That's very kind of you."

"Now let's hope there are no more accidents," she said as she got up and tested her legs.

"Yeah," said Dudley. "I'd really hate for anyone else in my new family to get hurt."

33

Harriet had been thinking hard. Odelia's words, even though she'd dismissed them at first, had returned to her when suddenly Max, Dooley and Brutus had gone missing for half an hour, only to return with Clarice in tow.

For a moment there, she'd actually panicked. She wasn't used to her boyfriend abandoning her like that—usually it was she who did the abandoning, not the other way around, and to see Brutus take off like that, without telling her what he was up to, had given her a big shock.

And so in his absence she'd started ruminating on Odelia's words. What had she said? Something about compassion? And how humans and pets who lost control over their bladders were basically more to be pitied than censored?

And so suddenly she'd seen this entire incident in a different light: Brutus and Dooley weren't the bad guys here —they were the victims! Victims… of their wonky bladders.

And so as they walked along the sidewalk, Clarice out in front, scanning left and right and generally taking her body-

PURRFECT SON

guarding duties very seriously, and Rambo behind them, generally looking extremely bored and wishing he were anywhere but there, she suddenly said, "Brutus, I think I owe you an apology."

"What?" said Brutus, visibly surprised.

"Yeah, I talked to Odelia about your condition, and I see now that I judged you too harshly. You, too, by the way, Dooley."

"Oh-kay," said Brutus cautiously, clearly wondering what the catch was.

"So now I'm thinking you two should probably get some professional help."

"Pro-professional… help?"

"I'm sure if you talk to Vena she'll be able to give you something for that dodgy bladder of yours. You're too young to let this kind of problem control your life, smoochie poo. And I know that Odelia suggested placing a plastic tub in the bedroom so you won't have this kind of… accident in the middle of the night, but just know there is a more permanent solution. One that will make your bladder behave again—just like it used to." And she proceeded to give her boyfriend a big smile of support.

"But… my bladder is just fine," said Brutus.

"My bladder is fine, too," said Dooley.

"I don't need to go to the doctor."

"Me, neither," said Dooley.

"Now Brutus, I know you like to act tough and all, but there really is no shame in this. There are many, many people, and plenty of pets, who suffer the same thing you two do."

"Suffer… what, exactly?" asked Brutus, wide-eyed now.

"Well, incontinence, of course. And I'm sure that if you just talk to Vena—"

"Incontinence!"

"What is incontinence, Max?" asked Dooley.

"It's when you have no control over your bladder. Or your bowels."

"But… I'm not incontinent!" Brutus cried.

"Now, now, pookie bear," said Harriet, contriving a look of compassion. "There's no sense denying the obvious. And no shame, you hear me? No shame whatsoever."

"I'm not ashamed—my bladder works perfectly fine, and so does everything else!"

"Oh, munchkin," said Harriet with a sigh. "I knew you'd react this way. Look, you don't have to act tough for my sake. I'll talk to Odelia and set up an appointment with Vena."

"What?!!!"

"And I want you to know you have my full support, my precious angel. My love muffin. My cuddle bear. I'll be right by your side throughout the whole procedure."

"But I'm not—"

"Oh, I know, chickadee. I know."

"But my bladder is perfectly—"

"Of course it is. Absolutely."

"But, Harriet!"

"It's all right, handsome. And I love you all the same—my incontinent honey bear."

"Can you please cut down on the blather?" asked Clarice annoyedly. "I can't focus."

"Yes, Clarice," said Harriet dutifully.

She wasn't entirely happy about this new situation, but it was better than being attacked by some pyromaniacal cat killer. And since she'd try to be more compassionate from now on, she could see that even though Clarice was all bluster and snide comments, underneath all that was a scared little pussy. At least she thought there was.

So she sidled up to Clarice now, and said, "Clarice, honey,

you don't have to act tough on my account, you know. I mean, it's perfectly fine to be yourself when I'm around."

"What are you talking about, toots?" asked Clarice, her eyes flitting all over the place, like one of those Secret Service agents running along the car with their president. All that was missing now were a pair of snazzy sunglasses and a wrist mic to mumble into.

"What I mean is that we're just girls together, you and I, and you can't fool me."

"Still don't have a clue what you're talking about."

"You can drop the act, Clarice. Underneath that tough exterior you're a sweet soul. I know that. And it's all right to let it out."

Clarice cut her a look that was anything but sweet. "I think you better get back in line now, before I give you a piece of my soul you won't like."

Doubts started to creep in when Harriet looked deeply into the wild cat's eyes and saw not a hint of sweetness there —only an interior that was as tough or even tougher than the exterior. "I just want you to know," she said, placing a paw on Clarice's shoulder, "that I care. I care about you, Clarice, I really do."

Clarice glanced down at the paw, then up at Harriet, and her expression darkened. "If you don't remove that paw right now you're going to lose it."

"W-what?"

"I'm going to cut you, Harriet. I'm going to cut you so bad you'll wish you were never born."

"But... you're supposed to protect me!" she cried, removing her paw as if from a burning stove, then quickly rejoined the others. "Clarice isn't nice," she announced with a pout. "I tried to be compassionate and she threatened me— actually threatened me!"

"I know," said Brutus. "And that's why she's the best bodyguard in Hampton Cove. No offense, Rambo."

"None taken," said the big dog, lumbering along. "Hey, where can we find some food around here? I'm starving."

34

We'd finally arrived at Wilbur Vickery's General Store, where our friend Kingman usually presides over the proceedings, and I was frankly eager to have a word with the voluminous cat. Often when we're starved for information Kingman is the one who can provide that telling clue.

And as luck would have it there seemed to be some kind of impromptu cat choir meeting taking place outside Wilbur's store: Kingman was there, of course, but also Buster, the barber's Main Coon, Tigger, the plumber's cat, Shanille, cat choir's conductor, Misty, the electrician's cat, Tom, the butcher's cat, Shadow, who belongs to Franklin Beaver, the guy who runs the hardware store, and Missy, the landscaper's tabby.

"Oh, hey, fellas," said Kingman when we joined the meeting. "Shanille here has some exciting news to share."

Shanille was positively glowing as she turned to us. "The mall is happening—it's actually happening! Father Reilly has been asked to bless the first stone and he said yes!"

"So is that good news or bad news?" I asked.

"Good news for me," said Clarice. "It means the downtown area of Hampton Cove will turn into a ghost town and the streets will be littered with garbage and there will be more rats than people around." She smiled an icy smile. "And I do love me a juicy rat."

"You love rats?" asked Buster.

"To eat, I mean," said Clarice with a distinctly cruel grin.

Buster shivered, and so did the rest of the small company.

"I'm sure you're exaggerating, Clarice," said Shanille. "The mall will attract plenty of tourists, and the downtown area will thrive and local businesses will boom!"

"Boom as in go bust, you mean," said Clarice.

"Oh, don't listen to this Gloomy Gus," said Shanille. "Father Reilly says it's going to be just great. A brand-new future for our town!"

"It also means that Tex is going to be rich," said Brutus. "He's got a plot of land the mall developers want to buy," he explained to the others.

"Ooh, so you're going to be loaded soon," said Kingman. "I wish Wilbur had thought of getting himself a piece of land when he had the chance. Then he could probably retire and we could move to Florida or some other place nice and warm."

"I thought you didn't like the heat?" I asked.

"I don't mind the heat as long as there are plenty of great-looking females around," said Kingman with a shrug. "And something tells me that Florida's got some of the finest females in the country."

"Oh, don't be so vulgar, Kingman," said Shanille reproachfully. "Besides, your human will be making a fortune soon, when all those tourists start coming into town."

"You think?" said Kingman, his face lighting up.

"Of course! This mall is going to put Hampton Cove on

the map. We're all going to be rich—not just Marge and Tex—everyone!"

"I want to be rich," said Tigger with a wistful smile. "Being rich sounds nice."

"The only one who's going to be rich is me," said Clarice. "Rich in rats!"

"Oh, Clarice, just go away," said Shanille, clearly not all that fond of the feral cat.

"I can't go away—I'm guarding this quartet of bozos."

Kingman turned to me. "So you took my advice? That's great, buddy!"

But Shanille appeared less than impressed, judging from the way the corners of her mouth had turned down. "Are you sure this is a good idea, Max?"

"Of course it's a good idea!" said Kingman. "It was my idea!"

"So... you've got a cat... guarding another cat?" asked Missy, who seemed confused.

"It sure beats a human having to guard a cat," said Kingman.

"That's true," Shadow agreed with a curious glance at Clarice.

"So how does this work, exactly?" asked Buster, giving his fur a lick.

"Well," I said, a little shamefacedly, "since we were attacked in our own attic Odelia has hired Rambo over there and then we ourselves have retained Clarice's services."

"So let me get this straight," said Shanille. "First you got Chase to guard you—a *human*. Then a *dog*, and now Clarice? How many bodyguards does a cat need?!"

"Oh, you're just jealous, Shanille," said Harriet snippily.

"Jealous! I'm stunned, that's what I am! Stunned! Since when does a cat ask a human to be their bodyguard—or a dog, for that matter? That's just... wrong on so many levels!"

"It is a little weird," Misty agreed.

"You know I can hear you, right?" said Rambo now, waddling up. "And for your information, this is just as awkward for me as it is for these guys. What do you think the Dog Guild is gonna say when they find out I'm guarding cats—cats, for crying out loud!"

I was making myself as small as I could. Clearly my reputation was hanging by a thread, and so was the reputation of my housemates. Shanille was probably right. No cat allowed themselves to be guarded by a human or a dog—or another cat. It wasn't done.

"Look, what we're actually here for," I said, deciding to change the subject before things got completely out of hand, "is to find out more about the death of Charlene Butterwick's uncle. He died yesterday morning, and Odelia wants to know if anyone of you might have seen something, or heard something?"

But my friends weren't so easily distracted. "Even if my life were in danger, the last thing I'd do was to entrust my life and safety to a dog," said Shanille, still harping on the same theme. "No offense, Mr. Rambo."

"None taken, Miss Shanille," said the big dog good-naturedly. I saw that he was staring intently at the bags of dog kibble Wilbur Vickery had on sale this week.

"So no one knows anything about Charlene's uncle?" I asked. "Nothing?"

"Come on, guys," said Clarice. "Let's get out of here. First rule of bodyguarding: never allow your charge to stay in the same place for too long. Gotta stay mobile!"

Frankly I didn't mind skedaddling, as Shanille and the others had now fully embraced the bodyguarding theme and were running with it. Even Kingman was starting to see the error of his ways when he suggested retaining Clarice's services as our protection detail.

And as we set paw for home, I felt slightly deflated. Not only weren't we getting anywhere with our investigation, but our assailant was still out there, and our reputations, such as they were, were now thoroughly being reduced to less than nothing.

"Don't worry, Max," said Rambo, as he waddled up next to me, leaving a trail of goo on the sidewalk. "They'll come around to this whole guard dog thing. A new concept always takes a while to catch on. But before you know it this will become the new craze, and then every cat in Hampton Cove will want a dog to guard them."

"You think so?"

"Oh, sure. It's always like that. Just look at the pogo stick. First people think it's weird, and then they embrace it and everybody wants one. Thing starts flying off the shelves."

I didn't want to tell him that comparing a dog to a pogo stick was probably not doing his species justice, but his words definitely sounded like music to my ears.

When you live in a small town like Hampton Cove, your reputation is everything, you see. And so I very much cared what other cats thought of me.

"Just you wait and see," said Rambo. "This time next month they'll all come knocking on my door, offering me purses of gold if I'll be their bodyguard." And to emphasize his words, he dropped a big glob of blubbery goo onto the sidewalk.

Somehow the gesture seemed to detract from the confidence he was exuding. Then again, I'm not well-versed in analyzing trends, and I've never used a pogo stick in my life, so what did I know?

"So are we there yet?" asked Rambo, his breathing a little labored, I thought.

"No, I'm afraid we're not an inch closer to figuring out

who might have killed Charlene's uncle—or even *if* he was killed," I said.

"I mean—are we home yet? I'm hungry."

And so I learned another valuable truth about dogs: some of them have a one-track mind. And that's not me being critical of my canine brethren. Merely stating a fact.

But lucky for Rambo we'd finally arrived home, and as we walked along the narrow stretch between the two houses belonging to our humans, suddenly I heard a loud scream. And when we raced to track the source of the scream, we came upon a grisly scene: Tex was lying on his back, and blood was streaming down his face.

"I'm hit!" he said. "Help me, I'm hit!"

35

"Oh, Dad—Daddy! What happened?"

Tex groggily glanced around, and as if through a haze saw his son come running out of the house. Dudley knelt down next to him.

"I've been hit," he repeated. "Someone shot me. Right… here…" He gestured vaguely in the direction of his head, then started feeling even woozier than before.

"Oh, Daddy, Daddy, please don't die," said Dudley. "We just found each other—please don't die on me now." He was sniffling and tears now flowed from Tex's own eyes, too.

"I'm sorry, Dudders," he croaked. "But they-they got me good this time. I think it's the end for me. Tell Marge… tell her I love her, will you? Tell her… I'm sorry."

And as if summoned by some unseen hand—or possibly the cats having told her about what had happened—his wife now came hurrying up to them.

"Tex!" she screamed. "Tex, no!"

"Goodbye, Marge," he said weakly. "This is the end for me. Tell Odelia… I love her…"

Just then, Odelia materialized, looking as stricken as the others were all feeling.

"Dad!" she said, her voice distinctly wobbly. "Daddy, no!"

"I'll always be up there… watching over you," he said, pointing heavenward with his final remaining ounce of strength. "Good… bye."

"Oh, will you stop whining, you sissy," suddenly a loud voice intruded upon his most tragic death scene. He frowned as he recognized his mother-in-law's voice.

"Vesta," he croaked. "Take care of… my family… will you?" He would have told her he loved her, but since he didn't, he didn't.

"It's just a flesh wound, you idiot!" And to show him she meant what she said, she pressed something very stinging to his ear.

"Ouch!" he said, jumping up. "What are you doing, you silly woman!"

"I'm disinfecting the tiny cut on your ear, you wimp," said Vesta, then held up a piece of metal and brought it in for his close inspection. "A piece of your lawnmower," she said. "How many times have I told you to buy yourself a new one? This piece of junk was always going to come apart sooner or later."

"Tex! She's right!" said Marge. "It's only a tiny flesh wound where the blade of that lawnmower hit you!"

He frowned as he took a closer look at that piece of blade Vesta had shoved under his nose. It looked very sharp indeed. "That thing cut me?" he asked.

"Yes, it did," said Vesta. "You're one lucky dude. This could have been your noggin," she added, pressing an antiseptic-soaked cotton ball to his ear and making him wince.

He scrambled into a sitting position and surveyed the scene: there the lawnmower was, now minus a part of its blade, and there the cat contingent sat, all eyeing him piteously. And next to him, his family: Marge, Vesta, Odelia and… his son Dudley.

"So I'm not going to die?" he asked finally.

"No, you're not!" said Odelia, and threw herself into his arms.

"Oh, you silly, silly man," said Vesta, but she was smiling as she said it.

"I don't get it," said Marge. "It's been one accident after another. First Ma falling down the stairs, then me electrocuting myself, and now this. What's going on?"

"And don't forget about my car breaking down," said Odelia. "Or the cats almost being burned alive yesterday."

"That was no accident," said Vesta.

"It's my fault," said Dudley suddenly, looking rueful. "Since I arrived in this family accidents started to happen."

"Oh, nonsense," said Tex, now pressing the cotton ball to his own ear. "Like Vesta said, that lawnmower was going to break down sooner or later, and that coffeemaker has seen better days, too, as has that old pickup of yours, Odelia. And as far as that runner is concerned, I screwed that thing into place myself… fifteen years ago!"

"We probably should replace it," said Marge, giving her mother an apologetic look.

"I'm just glad you guys are fine," said Odelia. "And accidents happen, Dudley," she added. "It's not your fault." She smiled at her brother, and it warmed Tex's heart to see both of his kids getting along so well. It's just the kind of thing a loving father likes to see.

"Let's just hope this was the last of the accidents," said Vesta. "I'm a tough old girl, but even I didn't enjoy tumbling down those stairs."

They all laughed at that, relief making them a little giddy, and even Tex was laughing along. And then Dudley suddenly said, "Is it just my imagination or is the number of cats growing in number? I thought you had four cats and now I see… five and a dog?"

"Oh, that's Clarice," said Odelia. "She's a street cat and she'll be keeping an eye on the others. And that's Rambo—he's a retired police dog and he'll be their guard dog for a while. At least until this cat killer is finally caught."

"I don't know what this place is coming to," said Marge. "Cat killers, if you please. Now who would try and kill our cats? You really have to be a sicko to try and do that."

"Yeah, only a real sicko would do that," Dudley agreed as he cast a curious look at Clarice, who stared right back at him, brazen as dammit, as was her habit.

Rambo, meanwhile, was already disappearing into the house, probably eager to get his nutrients in. Good thing that Tex was about to become a millionaire, he thought, because that dog was going to cost him an arm and a leg in dog chow if he kept this up.

"Where is Chase?" he asked, getting up from the freshly mown lawn with a groan.

"Still at work. He'll be here soon," said Odelia, supporting him.

"I'll do that," said Dudley, and took over from his sister. Tex proudly leaned on his son's arm. It felt good to have a son, he thought. And as they walked into the house he thought this was probably one of the proudest days of his life. Well, except that he'd just made a total fool of himself over that lawnmower accident, of course. Or that his wife had almost died by electrocution, or his mother-in-law had practically broken her neck falling down the stairs. Or that his daughter had almost died in a head-on collision.

But apart from that? Proudest day of his life. And then he suddenly stumbled, and hit his head against the kitchen table and the world as he knew it instantly turned dark.

36

"I don't trust that guy," said Clarice the moment Dudley and Tex were out of sight.

But since moments later Tex went down again and everyone convened in the kitchen to try and revive him, I momentarily forgot about her words.

Tex turned out to be all right, though, and when five minutes later he came to, he said he'd clumsily got tangled up in his own feet and hit his head against the kitchen table.

Against Tex's protestations Marge called a doctor, just to make sure he was all right and no permanent damage had been done, and by the time we all returned next door, Tex lay tucked into bed, sleeping the sleep of the dead—though hopefully not too dead!

"He's a bad one, that," said Clarice once we were all installed on the couch, with Odelia moving around in the kitchen preparing dinner.

"Who are you talking about, Clarice?" asked Harriet.

"That Dudley, of course. Who else? I can see it in his eyes. He's up to no good."

"He seems like a great kid," I said.

"He's very nice," Harriet chimed in. "Last night he even gave me some of that special pâté Marge likes to keep for special occasions."

"And he cleaned out our litter boxes and put some extra litter inside—the nice-smelling kind," said Brutus.

"He gave me a boost when I had trouble jumping on top of the couch," said Dooley.

"I don't care if he's the perfect boy scout," said Clarice. "I'm telling you now that he's bad news. Also, I'm pretty sure he tripped up Tex just now, causing him to hit his head."

"He did? I didn't see that," I said.

"That's because your eyes aren't as sharp as mine," said Clarice, making me bristle a little.

"My eyes are perfectly fine," I said.

"Your eyes may be fine, but Dudley's got you all bamboozled. And now you only see what he wants you to see. And that goes for the entire Poole family."

We let those words sink in for a moment, and just then Dudley walked in and said, "Need a hand, sis?"

He got a radiant smile in return from Odelia.

"No, that's all right, Dudley," she said. "Chase will be here any minute. It's his turn to cook tonight. I'm just making sure we've got all the ingredients for spaghetti."

"Chase only cooks spaghetti?" asked Dudley with a laugh.

Odelia made a comical face. "Don't laugh. It's his specialty."

"I like spaghetti. So if what you're saying is true, Chase is just my kind of guy."

"Won't you stay for dinner?"

"You don't mind?"

"No, of course not."

"Then sure," said Dudley, and took a seat at the kitchen counter.

And as he and his sister continued to shoot the breeze, I

saw Clarice study him all the while, never taking her eyes off him. And when Dudley glanced in her direction once or twice, her eyes narrowed, and her upper lip pulled back in a snarl. If Dudley was worried about this obvious display of enmity, he didn't show it.

Until suddenly he got up and walked over to Clarice. "So this one isn't yours?" he asked.

"No, Clarice doesn't belong to anyone," said Odelia. "But she drops by from time to time, so you might say I've half-adopted her."

"She's not very clean, is she?" he said, inspecting our friend more closely.

"That's what living on the street will do."

"Are you sure it's safe for your own cats? I mean, she's bound to be teeming with all kinds of parasites and other vermin. Fleas and lice and who knows what else."

"I hadn't thought about that," said Odelia, considering Clarice for a moment.

"Fleas and lice have a tendency to jump from one carrier to the next, sis. It only takes them a fraction of a second to contaminate Max and the others, not to mention your home. Do you really want to wake up tomorrow morning with your head full of lice?"

"Pet fleas or lice don't jump over to humans," said Odelia, but I could see that Dudley's comments had given her pause.

"If I were you I'd get rid of her," he said now, then shrugged. "Just my opinion. You do what you want, of course. Your cats, your decision."

Chase arrived home, then, and as the trio ate their dinner, I could see that this time it was Odelia who kept darting anxious glances at Clarice from time to time, no doubt wondering about all those fleas and lice and other parasites jumping all over her couches now, and all over her four cats.

"You have to watch out for this guy," Clarice repeated at a certain point.

"But why do you say that?" asked Harriet. "He looks perfectly nice to me."

"Because he reminds of my own human, that's why," said Clarice. "He has the exact same look in his eyes. And my own human was a sweetheart, or at least I thought he was, until one day he drove me into the woods, tied me to a tree, and left me to die."

"How did you escape, Clarice?" asked Dooley, interested, even though he'd heard the story many times before. "Is it true you had to gnaw off your own paw to get away?"

Clarice held up two perfectly fine paws. "No, Dooley. I don't know who invented that story, but that's definitely not what happened. Who'd want to gnaw off their own paw?"

"Oh," said Dooley, looking slightly disappointed.

"No, a kind-hearted couple happened to pass by the spot where my human left me, and rescued me. I would have stayed with them, but by then I was frankly over humans, so I ate my fill, said thank you very much, and I've been on my own ever since."

"Good for you," said Brutus with a nod.

Rambo, who'd been fast asleep, now woke up and yawned, causing a very foul smell to waft in our direction.

"What did I miss?" he asked.

"Clarice was just telling us how her human abandoned her and tied her to a tree," said Dooley excitedly. "But then a couple of very kind humans came by and saved her from certain death! Isn't that the most beautiful story you've ever heard, Rambo? I think I like it even better than the one about you gnawing off your own paw, Clarice."

"Oh, brother," Clarice muttered.

"I was once tied to a tree," said Rambo. "So I yanked that sucker out of the ground and ran off with it."

"You yanked a whole tree out of the ground?" asked Harriet.

"Yes, ma'am. Big tree, too. Just gave it a yank and that was it for Mr. Tree. Game over."

"I don't believe this," said Clarice, shaking her head.

"Well, you better believe it, cause that's what happened. And now if you'll excuse me, I think I'll have a bite to eat. I'm starting to feel faint. Hunger has that effect on me."

And he waddled off, leaving a trail of goo on Odelia's nice hardwood floor. It glistened.

37

"Look, I like her, too, Max, but Dudley is right. Who knows where Clarice has been—and I would never forgive myself if you guys came down with some bug that she's transmitted to you."

"I'm pretty sure no bug would dare to attach itself to Clarice," I said. "Or a parasite."

"It's all right, Max," said Clarice. "You don't have to defend me. If they want me gone, I'll go."

"I'm sorry, Clarice," said Odelia. "But you must understand that—"

"All humans are the same? No, yeah, I absolutely understand."

"Oh, please don't take it like that," said Odelia.

"Just forget about it," said Clarice, and walked out the pet flap and was gone.

"That wasn't very nice of you," I told my human.

"I'm sorry, Max," she said. "But I'm just doing it to protect you."

"Right," I said, and then followed in Clarice's wake, hoping I could still catch her. "Clarice! Hold up!" I yelled when I caught up with her at the end of our street. She turned and I could tell that Odelia's unexpected betrayal didn't sit well with the tough cat. "I'm so sorry," I said. We were sitting under a streetlamp, and its diffuse light lit up Clarice's mottled fur. I didn't see any sign of any parasites, though, or fleas or whatever.

"I knew this was going to happen," she said. "This Dudley kid sees me as a threat. Cause I'm on to him, and you're not. So he got rid of me—plain and simple. And Odelia, that gullible fool, allowed herself to be played for a sucker."

"But I don't understand. What could Dudley possibly have to gain by getting rid of you. What does he want?"

"Haven't you figured it out yet, Max? He wants to destroy you."

"Destroy us? What do you mean?"

"The accidents, dummy! I'll bet that's all him."

I shook my head. "But that can't be. He's been nothing but kind to us. And Tex is so happy that he finally has a son."

"Oh, Max," said Clarice with a sigh. "Look, this really is none of my business, but I care about you, so I'm going to tell you this once, and then I'm out of here." She fixed me with an intense look. "Watch out for this Dudley kid. Okay? Watch your back, and watch your humans' back."

"But…"

"I gotta go. Take care of yourself, and thanks for sticking your neck out just now." She smiled. "No one has ever stood up for me like that before. I appreciate it, big buddy."

"Don't go, Clarice. I'm sure if I just talk to Odelia—"

"Don't sweat it, Max. I'm used to being screwed over by humans. See ya around." And with these words, she walked away.

And as I returned to the house, thinking about everything Clarice had said, I suddenly saw a car pull over in front of Marge and Tex's home. Dudley then came walking out, talked to whoever was driving the car, and accepted a package from the driver, then the car took off before I reached the house and could see who was behind the wheel.

And by the time I arrived, Dudley had already returned indoors.

Could Clarice be right? Could Dudley be a threat to us and to our humans? But why? What was he playing at?

And so it was a slightly downcast Max who walked in through the pet flap again, and installed myself on my favorite spot on my favorite couch.

"Is she gone?" asked Dooley sadly.

"Yeah, she's gone," I said, just as sadly.

"I like Clarice. I like her very much."

"Me, too," I said. "I think she's just great."

"And I don't think she's got parasites, Max."

"No, I don't think so either, Dooley."

Brutus and Harriet had already returned next door, and were probably getting ready to go to bed. With Chase being relieved of guard duty, and Clarice having been dismissed, that only left Rambo as our guard dog, and Odelia didn't think it was a good idea to entrust the safety of her cats to the old dog, so she'd told us there was to be no cat choir tonight.

It wasn't fair, I thought, but then I'm just a cat, right? And clearly Odelia wasn't going to take my advice, as the Clarice incident had clearly shown.

So I simply closed my eyes and decided to take a long nap —preferably until this whole ordeal had somehow sorted itself out—or longer.

And I probably would have made good on my promise if I hadn't been awakened in the middle of the night by the sound of the pet flap flapping not once but twice. And suddenly Harriet and Brutus materialized in front of me.

"You have to come, Max," said Harriet, sounding worried. "It's Marge. She's fallen into some kind of coma."

They were words that had the effect of making me jump off that couch and immediately follow my friends, with Dooley right behind me.

Moments later we were in the upstairs bedroom, where Tex was bent over his wife's prostrate body, trying to revive her. Outside, the sounds of an approaching ambulance could be heard, and Vesta, who'd been hovering nearby, now hurried down the stairs to open the front door for the paramedics.

"Marge!" said Tex, extremely distraught. "Please, Marge, wake up!"

But Marge didn't respond. What was more, she was white as a sheet, and looked as if she'd already passed on to meet her maker.

"Oh, dear," said Harriet in hushed tones. "This is bad, isn't it? This is very, very bad."

And immediately Clarice's words came back to me, and when I turned and saw Dudley hovering in the doorway, looking on, I thought I saw a small smile flit across his handsome face. Then, when he saw me looking at him, he gave me a wink, and put his finger to his lips in the universal gesture of 'Keep quiet…'

Oh, dear. So Clarice had been right all along!

38

It was only when the ambulance siren stopped right outside the house that Odelia woke up with a start. She swung her feet from between the covers and hurried to the spare bedroom, which had a window looking out onto the street. When she saw that the ambulance was parked right outside her parents' house, her heart skipped a beat.

And then she was crying, "Chase! Wake up!" and was thundering down the stairs, hurrying next door. As she flitted through the kitchen door, she almost fell over Harriet.

"I was just coming to get you," said the Persian. "It's your mom. I think she's… dead."

"Oh, God, no!" she said, and arrived upstairs just in time to see the paramedics strap her mother onto a stretcher and then carry her downstairs.

"What happened?" she asked her dad, who looked as white as her mom did, maybe even whiter.

"I don't know," said Dad. "She… started convulsing—woke me up. And then suddenly she breathed a long rattling sigh and… was gone."

"Oh, Dad! Don't tell me she's…"

"I managed to bring her back, but she's practically unresponsive." He shook his head. "Looks like catatonic shock to me."

"But how?"

"I don't know, honey. Could be something she ate that she responded badly to, or something she drank…"

"But you both ate the same thing, right?"

"We all ate the same thing," said her grandmother. "And drank the same thing, too."

"Mom does get up sometimes, in the middle of the night," said Odelia. "And she usually makes herself a glass of warm milk, right? Could that be…"

"I don't know," said her dad, and then he was following the paramedics. He turned, and said, "I'm going to the hospital. If you want to come, better come now."

Chase, who'd arrived at the bottom of the stairs, raked his fingers through his shaggy mane. "What's going—Marge? What the hell!"

"Drive my daughter to the hospital, will you, son? "said Tex, placing a hand on Chase's shoulder, then hurrying off so he could ride along in the ambulance.

Chase glanced up at Odelia, and she must have looked extremely distraught, for his face fell.

"Let's get out of here," said Gran, and gave Chase a pointed look. "You drive. I'll call Alec and tell him to meet us at the hospital."

"If you want, I can drive," said Dudley.

Gran gave him a grateful smile. "Thanks, Dudley. That's very kind of you. Now let's go, people. And don't forget to lock up the house. There will be no neighborhood watch tonight."

"I think they may have forgotten about us, Max," said Dooley as we watched the car drive off, Dudley behind the wheel and the rest all strapped in tight.

"Yeah, I think you're right," I said.

We'd thought they would surely take us along to the hospital, but now it looked like they'd totally forgotten about us.

"It's only natural," said Harriet. "They're not thinking straight—none of them are."

"I hope Marge is all right," said Brutus. "I like Marge. In fact I think she's probably the best of them."

"Yeah, she is," I agreed.

I wondered if I should tell the others about what I saw, then figured it was my duty to. So I told them about what Clarice had said, and also about the scene I'd witnessed when I got back from saying goodbye to Clarice, and even Dudley's eerie little smile.

"Maybe Clarice is right," said Harriet now. "If she says she saw Dudley trip up Tex, that's what must have happened. I mean, why would she lie about a thing like that?"

"And you say this person gave something to Dudley?" asked Brutus.

"Yeah, I was too far away to see what it was, but it looked like a small parcel."

"Does Amazon Prime do midnight deliveries?" asked Harriet.

"I doubt it," I said.

"But… why would Dudley try to kill Marge?" said Dooley, and we all looked at him, as he'd said what we'd all been thinking, and now the words hung heavy in the air.

"I don't know, Dooley," I said. "But it's too much of a coincidence for this to happen the day after he moved in."

"Too much of a coincidence for all these accidents to happen all of a sudden," said Harriet. "Odelia's car, Vesta falling down the stairs, Tex almost slicing off his ear, Marge getting electrocuted…"

"What is this guy playing at?" asked Brutus the million-dollar question. "What does he want?"

Suddenly Rambo came waddling through the hole in the dividing hedge, looking sleepy.

"What's going on?" he asked in his big, booming voice. "Did I miss something?"

"Rambo, you're a police dog, right?" I said.

"And you better believe it," he said with a yawn as he sank down on his haunches and started licking his ass.

"What do you make of Dudley?"

He shrugged. "Looks like a nice kid."

"What if we told you that he might have just killed Marge?" said Brutus.

He frowned at this. "Killed Marge? You mean Marge is dead?"

"Not yet, but it's not looking good," I said.

"Oh, Max," said Dooley. "I don't want Marge to die. She's so nice!"

"I know, Dooley. I know."

Rambo frowned some more, which caused his eyes to disappear into the swaths of skin that formed his face. "Well, if he did try to kill Marge, he probably did it when he dumped those drops into her milk."

We all stared at the big dog. "What?!" I asked, once I'd recovered from the shock.

"Yeah, I saw him through the kitchen window. Dumping some kind of drops in a glass of milk, then turn around and offer it to Marge. They were laughing and talking so nice I just figured he'd given her something to help her sleep."

"Maybe that was the parcel he received," said Harriet, turning to me.

"Must be," I said.

So there you had it. Dudley had tried to kill Marge. But why? And, most importantly, how were we ever going to convince our humans that Dudley was the bad guy?

39

The ambulance raced along the deserted streets, Dudley driving the car that carried Odelia, Chase and Gran, following right in the ambulance's wake.

It didn't take them long to arrive at the hospital, which was located one town over, in Happy Bays. As luck would have it, Tex's friend and colleague Denby Jennsen was the duty doctor, and immediately he and his team started working on Odelia's mom.

Meanwhile, the rest of the family were left nervously pacing the waiting room, anxious for some news.

Dudley made himself useful by fetching coffee and sugary snacks. He seemed to be least affected by the terrible events as they unfolded. A rock amid all of the turmoil.

Odelia felt grateful that he was there, providing some much-needed support for her dad, who looked devastated by his wife's sudden collapse and brush with death.

Suddenly a familiar figure dropped by in the form of Uncle Alec, followed by Charlene. They'd both clearly been fast asleep, as Uncle Alec's few remaining hairs stood akimbo, and Charlene's own curly blond tresses were plastered to the side of her face.

"Any news on my sister?" asked Uncle Alec the moment they swept into the room.

Odelia shook her head sadly. No news. Not yet.

"How did this happen?" asked her uncle as he took a seat next to her and Chase.

"I have no idea," she said. "Maybe something she ate—food poisoning?"

"Oh, honey," said Charlene, as she took Odelia's hands in hers and squeezed.

And so they sat for a while, trying to keep their nerves under control.

"Where are the cats?" suddenly asked Gran.

"I-I totally forgot about them," said Odelia.

"So they're all home alone?"

"They've got Rambo to keep an eye on them," she said, understanding her grandmother's meaning perfectly. With this cat killer on the loose, even the house wasn't safe for them.

"I'm sure your cats will be fine," said Dudley, proving himself to be a real pillar of strength to the family in this, their darkest hour.

"I shouldn't have kicked out Clarice," said Odelia now.

"Wait, you kicked out Clarice?" asked Gran. "Why?"

Odelia shrugged. "Dudley made a valid point about Clarice bringing all kinds of parasites and vermin into the house, and even infesting our own cats. So I put her out."

Gran directed a not-so-friendly look at Dudley, who pretended not to notice. "That was probably the worst kind of advice he could have given you," said the old lady.

"I know, I know," said Odelia, rubbing her eyes. It hadn't been her best decision ever, and she now felt thoroughly bad about asking Clarice to leave. She felt even worse about forgetting to bring along her cats now. But in the commotion after finding her mother unresponsive, she'd completely lost her head.

"Clarice will be fine," said Chase now, patting her hand. "And so will your cats."

"What's taking them so long?" Dad said. "This is a bad sign, right? It can't be good."

"You tell me," said Uncle Alec. "You're the doctor, Tex, so you should know."

"Okay," said Dad, nodding. "So let's just assume it's a good sign. A very good sign." And he went right on pacing, this time taking a turn along the hospital corridor.

"So how's the project?" asked Odelia. She had zero interest in the mall project, but anything would do to take her mind off her mom's condition. "Is the mall happening?"

But Charlene shook her head. "The developers called me this afternoon. The results came back from a feasibility study they ordered six months ago and it wasn't good. According to the study, building and operating a second mall in the area simply isn't economically viable so close to the Hampton Keys mall, so they've taken a radical decision and they're going to drop the project entirely. Cut their losses while they can."

"What, no mall?" asked Chase.

"No mall," said Charlene, then shrugged. "Maybe it's for the best. I wasn't a big proponent of the project, and I don't think I would have gotten a majority in the council."

"The mall isn't happening?" suddenly asked Dudley, looking stunned.

"No, it's been shelved by the developers," said Charlene. "Not economically viable."

"But... so Tex's plot of land..."

"Oh, Tex will definitely be able to sell," said Charlene. "But not at the inflated prices the developers were willing to offer. I think we'll go back to our housing development idea. Turn the area into a great neighborhood for young families. Much better that way."

"But… no!" said Dudley, looking stricken. He'd gone red in the face and was striking the palm of his hand with his fist.

"It's all right, Dudley," said Odelia. "Mom and Dad didn't really need that money."

"Though it would have been nice," said Gran.

It didn't matter anyway—not if Mom wouldn't make it. Immediately Odelia tamped down on the thought. Mom had to make it. She just had to.

And just then, Denby Jennsen appeared, looking tired but radiant. "It's all right," he announced happily. "Marge will be fine." They all got up and crowded around the doctor. "Looks like a case of food poisoning to me," he said. "Though we'll have to wait for the lab results to know for sure. But she's doing great—if you want you can go and see her now."

They didn't need to be told twice, and immediately were off in the direction indicated.

"Mom!" said Odelia the moment they set foot in her mother's room. "Oh, Mom!" And then she was hugging her mom, who looked as if she'd been put through the wringer.

"I'm okay," said Odelia's mother, her voice a little weak.

"What happened?" asked Uncle Alec.

"I don't know," said Mom. "I woke up in the middle of the night with a tummy ache that just seemed to get worse and worse. And then suddenly I must have lost consciousness. And when I woke up I was right here, in the hospital." She smiled. "So it's me who should be asking you guys what happened."

"Oh, honey," said Tex, his face teary. "I knew you'd pull through. I just knew it."

"Of course I pulled through. I'm a doctor's wife, aren't I? I'm in good hands."

Tex nodded, and then he was blubbering like a baby.

The scene was a happy one, but it made Odelia wonder what was going on. First this long string of accidents they'd been subjected to and now this? What was happening?

And that's when she noticed that Dudley… was gone.

40

"We have to warn them!" said Harriet.

"But how?" I said. "They'll never believe us. They think Dudley is the greatest thing since apple pie."

"Then we go on a hunger strike," said Harriet decidedly. "They'll have to listen to us if we simply stop eating."

"A hunger strike!" said Brutus, who likes his three square meals a day.

"It's the only way, twinkle toes. People don't like it when their cats stop eating. It makes them go nuts."

"I'll go nuts if I can't eat."

"It's a small sacrifice to make, sweet cheeks."

"I think it's a great idea," said Rambo. "You go on your hunger strike, and in the meantime I'll make sure this Dudley character doesn't come anywhere near you." And as he said this, I saw he was eyeing our respective bowls eagerly.

"Oh, no," I said. "If we're going on a hunger strike you're going on a hunger strike, too."

"But I'm not even part of the family!" said Rambo.

"You're part of this family now, Rambo. So you're striking right along with the rest of us."

"So how do we do this?" asked Brutus reluctantly.

"Simple," said Harriet. "We stop eating."

"But aren't we going to die if we stop eating?" asked Dooley. "Cats need to take regular nourishment or else they die," he explained.

"We can do without food for a couple of days," said Harriet. "Besides, I'm sure that our humans will cave pretty quickly. They wouldn't want to have our deaths on their conscience."

"So maybe we should stop drinking, too?" said Dooley. "I already did it once, and it was fine."

"You only stopped drinking for a couple of hours," I pointed out. "Now we'd stop drinking for possibly days, and I don't think that's a good idea. No food for a couple of days is fine, but no water? That's bad."

"You mean we'd die?"

"Yes, Dooley. If we don't drink, we'll die for sure, from dehydration."

"But I don't want to die, you guys."

"Look, we're not going to die, all right?" said Harriet, who wasn't a big fan of all this backtalk. "We're simply going to tell them that we're on a hunger strike, and that's it."

Brutus's eyes lit up. "Oh, I get it! So we *tell* them we're not eating, but secretly we'll keep on eating right along!"

"No, Brutus," said Harriet primly. "We're not going to touch our bowls."

"But... for how long?"

She threw up her paws. "How should I know? For as long as it takes!"

"Gandhi used to go on hunger strikes," said Dooley, clearly having done some research into the guy since Brutus had mentioned him. "Gandhi liked to go on hunger strikes all the time. And he never died."

"Oh, Dooley," said Harriet with a heavy sigh.

Brutus swallowed away a lump. He still seemed uncomfortable with the whole prospect. "Dooley?" he asked quietly, nudging my friend. "Is there nourishment in pee? I mean, you said this Gandhi fellow doesn't eat, and I know for a fact he likes to drink his own pee, so the guy must be onto something, right? Does he live around here? Maybe we should go talk to him?"

"Oh, Brutus," said Harriet with an expressive eyeroll.

And just when we'd finally decided on our next course of action, suddenly a car pulled over outside, and we all hurried into Marge and Tex's front room to see if our humans had arrived home already.

Much to our surprise, though, it wasn't our humans but… Dudley, arriving in a cab.

He seemed in a hurry, too, for he came stalking up the little footpath to the house, and let himself in with the latchkey Tex had proudly given this newly acquired son of his.

"What do we do!" Brutus said as we heard the key turn in the lock.

"I don't know!" I said, and then we all turned to Rambo, our resident police dog, but the latter simply shrugged.

"Don't look at me, fellas. I'm retired."

"Oh, Rambo!" said Harriet with a loud groan.

But then Dudley was already entering the house, and running up the stairs.

"What is going on?" asked Brutus as we listened to the kid stomping around upstairs. "What is he up to?"

It didn't take long for us to realize what was going on, for moments later Dudley reappeared, this time carrying a duffel bag, and making for the front door again. And he probably would have left if he hadn't changed his mind at the sight of the small, slightly dilapidated goatherd figurine Tex and Marge like to keep in the front room.

Dudley glanced at the thing, then up at the painting of a gnome Tex has got hanging over the mantel, and changed course.

He stepped into the room, grabbed the figurine and dumped it into his suitcase. Then he took the painting from the wall and was about to abscond with it when Rambo sneezed.

Yes, dogs can sneeze, and so can cats.

Dudley looked up, startled, and it didn't take him long to discover our presence behind the couch.

"Well, look at you," he said, and I saw he had a very nasty expression on his face as he said it. "Four cats and one stupid old dog." And as he stared down at us, suddenly he got a certain gleam in his eyes that I didn't like to see there. It was the kind of gleam that spells doom. Probably the same kind of gleam that often comes into Dracula's eyes just before he decides to sink his teeth into the neck of another innocent young maiden.

"Max?" said Dooley.

"Yes, Dooley?"

"I don't like the way Dudley is looking at us!"

"Me, neither!"

"You know what?" said the floppy-eared young man, "I think it's time for me to finish what I started." And he kicked the door to the room closed with his foot. He then expertly picked me up by the scruff of the neck, the procedure giving me a distinct sense of déjà-vu, and dumped me into the couch. I probably should explain that Marge and Tex's couch is one of those couches with a hidden compartment inside, where they like to store stuff they don't need, such as: doilies, old curtains… And now yours truly, too!

In short order, he rounded up Harriet, Dooley and Brutus, and dumped us all in the couch, then slammed the thing shut, the couch springs and hinges squeaking creepily!

"You know? This reminds me of something," said Brutus suddenly.

"Yeah, me too," I said.

And when suddenly I smelled smoke, I knew exactly what it reminded me of. Yesterday morning in the attic, when Motorcycle Man had tried to set us on fire!

41

"I'd dump you in there, too, but you're too big and stupid, you old mutt," we heard Dudley say, presumably addressing our mighty guard dog.

"Max! Why did you let him catch you?" said Harriet, indignation clear in her voice.

"Why did *you* let him catch you!" I returned.

"Because it all happened so fast! And besides, he's Tex's son."

"But we already decided he's up to no good," I said. "So why did we let ourselves be duped like this?"

"I think because deep down we find it hard to believe that Tex's son would do a thing like this," said Dooley. "I think deep down we all want to believe that Dudley is a good person. That deep down he loves us just like the others do, and that deep down he means well. I think deep down—"

"Oh, will you stop it with your 'deep down' already!" Harriet cried. "We're in deep doo-doo right now, if you hadn't noticed!"

She was right. The flames were licking at the couch that was our new home, and if I know anything about couches it is that they are not flame-resistant. In fact you could probably argue that the modern couch is a fire accelerant, with all the synthetic materials it's made of.

"Let's put our backs into it, you guys," I said. "On the count of three, and push!"

And push we did, but the couch wasn't budging—not a single inch!

"Again! Push!" I said, feeling like a football coach leading his team to victory.

But no dice. Obviously Dudley had put some heavy object on top of the couch, preventing our escape.

"Maybe we can scratch our way out?" Brutus suggested.

And so we hurriedly started looking for the couch's weak spots. Unfortunately a couch, in case you didn't know, consists of particleboard, covered with polyurethane foam, covered with upholstery. Polyurethane and upholstery are no match for four highly motivated cats with very sharp claws and teeth, but particleboard is. So we could scratch all we wanted to, but we'd never manage to make it through. At least not in time to save our lives.

"So we just wait," said Harriet. "We wait until the fire does the work for us, and then we escape."

It sounded a lot like her plan from the day before, when we were locked inside that old chest in the attic. If her idea had sounded too good to be true then, it certainly sounded like the lousiest idea I'd ever heard now. But since I didn't want to undermine morale, I kept quiet. After all, what was the alternative: to announce to my friends that we would all soon be burnt to a crisp?

The smoke was coming in through the cracks already, and that orange glow was intensifying, as was the heat surrounding us.

"Max?" said Dooley.

"Mh?"

"I just want to say that you're the best friend a cat could ever hope to find. And if we don't make it—"

"Don't talk like that, Dooley."

"If we don't make it, I just want to say that it was an honor to be your friend."

"It was an honor for me, too, buddy."

"I have a confession to make," suddenly said Harriet.

Oh, no—not again with the confessions!

"I peed in all of your bowls last night," she said, sounding contrite.

"Peed in our bowls?" asked Brutus. "But why?"

"Because you peed in mine, okay?! So I peed in yours. And now I realize it was childish of me, and petty, and I'm sorry."

"I *accidentally* peed in your bowl," said Brutus. "And so did Dooley."

"And I did it on purpose, so there. Now can we put this whole peeing episode behind us already and move on?"

"You mean to say I actually drank your—"

"I said let's move on!"

"Look, if it's good enough for Gandhi," Dooley began, but the rest of his words were lost when suddenly the entire couch seemed to explode in a roar of fire and smoke!

On closer inspection, the roar hadn't been produced by the couch but by… Rambo!

And as we all stared into the face of the old bulldog, suddenly another familiar face hove into view: Clarice!

"What are you waiting for?" she said. "The bus? Get out of there already, will you? Move it!"

We didn't need to be told twice, and jumped out of the burning couch as fast as our legs could carry us!

And as we looked back, we saw that it wasn't just the couch that was on fire, but the carpet, too, and even one of those nice piecrust tables Marge is so fond of.

"Now let's put out this fire," said Clarice, proving herself a great fire chief.

"And how are we supposed to do that?" asked Harriet.

"Just follow my lead," said Clarice, and started to pee on the flames!

"I can do that," said Brutus, and took up position next to Clarice and started relieving himself.

Now I can tell you that cats are smallish animals, and our bladders are equally limited in size, as is the contents they can hold. So our urinary contributions didn't do much to fight those flames. It actually took that big bulldog Rambo to really make a difference. Whereas our little trickles had merely made that fire laugh in our faces, once Rambo opened the floodgates, those same belligerent flames didn't stand a chance!

And so by the time a car pulled up outside, and moments later the entire family Poole came charging in, what they found were the smoldering remnants of a couch, a carpet and a piecrust table and five cats and a dog performing a victory lap.

"What's that smell?" asked Gran. "Like a combination of smoke and… cat pee."

"And dog pee!" I cried. "Don't forget about all that beautiful, beautiful dog pee!"

And I reciprocated Rambo's high five with an even higher five of my own.

42

"Wha-what happened?" Tex said as he took in the devastation of his once immaculate front room.

"Dudley did this," said Max. "He tried to set us on fire—again. But not before he stole your goatherd figurine—the one you glued back together—and your gnome painting."

Odelia dutifully translated Max's words for those unable to understand him, drawing gasps of shock from Uncle Alec, Charlene and of course her dad.

"My son did this?" asked Dad, flabbergasted.

"Um, Tex," said Uncle Alec, placing a large hand on Odelia's dad's shoulder. "I just got a text from Abe Cornwall. I'm sorry to have to tell you this, but I had the lab run a DNA test and the result came back negative. Which means that Dudley... he isn't yours, buddy."

"About that," said Dad, giving his brother-in-law a very stern look. "I've been meaning to talk to you. I mean, doing a DNA test behind my back— Wait, what did you just say?"

"Dudley Checkers? He's not yours."

"Dudley isn't my son?!" Dad cried, staggering a little.

"I knew it!" said Gran.

"But… he looks just like me! My spitting image!"

"No, he doesn't," said Mom, who was recovering fast from her attack of food poisoning.

"Oh, and one other thing," said Max. "Rambo saw Dudley put something in Marge's milk. And I saw him receive a suspicious package just before. So I think it's safe to say that Dudley tried to kill Marge."

"What?!" Marge cried. She turned to her husband. "Your son tried to poison me!"

"He's not my son," said Dad defensively.

"I knew it!" Gran repeated.

"And Clarice saw how Dudley tripped up Tex and made him knock his head against the kitchen table," Harriet said now.

"And I'm pretty sure he probably was to blame for those other accidents, too," said Max.

"We put out the fire with our pee," Dooley announced happily. "Though Rambo peed the most."

"This is too much," said Gran, shaking her head. "And all under the nose of my watch." She pointed a finger at her son-in-law. "Your son tricked my watch, Tex! He tricked us!"

"He's not my son!" said Dad.

"So where is he?" asked Uncle Alec. "We need to stop him before he leaves town."

"I don't know," said Max. "He set us on fire and then he skedaddled."

Odelia faithfully played translator again, causing her uncle and her boyfriend to share a look of concern.

And then they both sprang into action, grabbing their respective phones and hurrying out of the house to see if they couldn't catch up with Dudley.

"Oh, no, you don't," said Gran, and took out her phone, too. "The watch will catch him!" And then she was off, too.

Odelia cast a glance at her cats and their guard dog and they all gave her a nod of agreement.

"We'll catch him," Max announced.

Odelia then crouched down next to Clarice. "I'm so sorry, honey," she said. "I guess I allowed myself to be bamboozled by Dudley, too. Can you ever forgive me?"

Clarice gave her a cold look. "Forgive you? Maybe. But I'll never forget." But then she grinned, and said, "Of course I'll forgive you, Odelia. And now let's get the bastard!"

So while Mom and Dad surveyed the devastation that Dudley's actions had caused to the house, three teams started what is commonly termed a dragnet: the police department, led by Uncle Alec and Chase, the local neighborhood watch, led by Gran, and a troupe of cats, led by... no one in particular.

"He can't have gotten far," said Odelia as she glanced up and down the street.

"I wouldn't be so sure," said Max. "He arrived in a cab, and I'm pretty sure he kept the cab waiting, so he's probably on his way to New York by now, or wherever he's going."

Odelia nodded, and got busy calling the different cab companies that covered Hampton Cove. She got lucky with the third one, but unlucky in that she didn't have her pickup, but lucky again when her grandmother came driving up, Scarlett riding shotgun. Gran rolled down the window and yelled, "Wanna ride with the watch, honey?"

"I thought you'd never ask," said Odelia, and soon she was filing into the car, followed by five cats and one dog, causing Scarlett to screw up her face and yell, "So smelly!"

But then Gran put her foot down on the accelerator and they were all thrown back against the seats.

"Where are we going?" asked Gran after a moment.

"He's heading to New York," Odelia said. "In a cab. And I've got the cab's number."

"Better tell your uncle," said Gran. "So he can call the cab company and tell the cab driver that he's got a fugitive in the back of his cab."

So Odelia did as she was told, and as they took the on-ramp to I-495, the Long Island Expressway, suddenly two squad cars joined them: one was Chase's, the other one Uncle Alec's, and so now the three teams were organizing a joint pursuit.

"I like this," said Brutus. "Almost like being in an action movie."

"My money is on your grandmother," said Clarice. "She clearly got the skills."

Odelia didn't think her gran had the skills, but what she certainly had was a lack of respect for the rules and regulations covering road safety, which gave her the edge.

And as they were zooming along the road, Odelia did some quick thinking. "So if Dudley tried to kill Mom, and Dad, and you, Gran—and me, with that car crash… he must have had a reason, right? And seeing as he left the hospital and packed his bags the moment Charlene announced that the mall project was scrapped, I'm assuming it must had something do with those millions he thought Mom and Dad were coming into."

"So he sweet-talked his way into our family," said Gran. "And tried to get rid of us one by one, hoping to lay his hands on that money?"

"That's what it looks like."

"The bastard," said Scarlett. "Wait till I get my hands on that rotten kid."

"No, wait till I get my hands on that no-good kid," growled Gran.

"Let's just try to catch him first, shall we?" Odelia suggested. "And not get ourselves killed in the process—Gran, watch it!" she added when Gran practically rear-ended a truck she apparently felt should get out of her flight path.

Odelia had Clarice on her lap, and was tickling the cat behind the ears, causing her to purr happily.

"You know?" said Clarice. "When you kicked me out I just figured it was par for the course—just another nasty human. But you're not like most humans, Odelia. You and your family? You're all right. And I just hate that kid for what he put you through."

"I'm the one to blame," said Odelia. "I should have done my due diligence. Who lets a person into their home, into their life, believing the stories they tell, without seeing if they really are who they say they are? I really dropped the ball on this one. Big time."

"I didn't like him from the start," said Gran, shaking her head as she sat hunched over the wheel, her foot all the way down to the metal, the engine a high whine.

"That's because you don't like anyone," said Scarlett as she checked her lipstick in the little visor mirror.

"Not true. I like you!"

"That's what you say."

"No, I really do!"

"Well, I don't like you." When Gran's jaw fell, Scarlett laughed. "I'm kidding! You're my buddy, buddy. And now will you please keep your eyes at the road, for Christ's sakes?"

"I wonder how Dudley knew about Mom and Dad's piece of land, though, and the mall development," said Odelia.

"We're about to find out," said Gran, and gestured with her head to a cab that had shown up in front of them—its taillights glowing in the darkness, the Taxi sign on the roof drawing them in like a homing beacon.

And before Odelia could tell her grandmother to play this cool, Gran was already leaning on the horn.

"Just rear-end him," said Scarlett.

"No, don't rear-end him!" said Odelia.

"Just hit him, Vesta—hit him!"

"Don't hit him!"

"She's going to kill us, Max," said Dooley sadly. "And we're not going to be able to pee our way out of this one."

"I'll just give him a little nudge, shall I?" said Gran, her tongue between her lips in utter concentration. "Bend that fender?"

"Get the sucker!" said Scarlett, clearly not the good influence on Gran that Odelia had thought she was.

Gran had sped up, and was now alongside the cab. The driver was glancing over, and making circular motions with his finger against his temple, and yelling something Odelia couldn't hear. And then she saw Dudley, and her so-called brother did not look pleased to see her.

"Just hit him!" said Scarlett. "Do it the watch way!"

But luckily for them, a police siren suddenly sounded behind them, as Uncle Alec and Chase had finally caught up with them after the crazy chase. And the cab driver quickly pulled over to the shoulder of the road.

"Oh, bummer!" said Gran, who'd just yanked the wheel to force the other car off the road. So instead she just parked in front of the cab, then backed up so their fenders touched, making sure the cab driver couldn't pull a fast one on her and get away.

"Why does your son always have to go and spoil the fun?!" Scarlett cried.

Odelia, though, heaved a sigh of relief, and so did five cats and one dog.

And as they got out of the car, Odelia saw to her surprise that Dudley was making a run for it!

And soon five humans, five cats and one dog were in hot pursuit of the prodigal son.

Scarlett soon dropped out of the impromptu race, as her

high heels weren't exactly conducive to this kind of frenetic activity. And then Gran had to give up, too.

"Stitch in my side!" the old lady yelled. "Go get him, hun!"

Uncle Alec was the next one to give up, and then it was just Chase and Odelia, and of course the entire pet contingent.

Dudley kept darting anxious glances over his shoulder.

"Give it up, Dudley!" Chase shouted.

"Get away from me!" Dudley screamed.

"Just stop!" said Odelia. "There's nowhere for you to go!"

"Leave me alone!"

Suddenly Rambo, of all pets, seemed to have found his second wind, for he came bounding up from the rear, and as Odelia watched on, he raced up to the fugitive, and before Dudley knew what was happening, the giant Bulldog tackled him from behind!

And then five cats were upon the kid, with Clarice, especially, digging her claws in.

And by the time Odelia and Chase arrived, their hot pursuit had turned into a rescue mission, as Odelia's pets clearly weren't holding back now that they'd got their guy.

"Help!" said Dudley as he tried to fend off the cat frenzy. "Heeeeelp meeeeeee!"

"I told you to stop," said Odelia, and had to physically drag Clarice off the guy. "That's enough," she said, and her cats all downed weapons. Rambo, still sitting on the man's back, had made himself comfortable, and produced a sonorous but happy bark.

"He's asking permission to bite," said Max.

"No—no biting!" said Odelia.

Rambo barked some more.

"And now he's asking permission to drool."

"Drool?"

And without further ado, Rambo started drooling all over

the back of Dudley's head. Soon the kid was looking like a drowning victim. And as he spat out the drool, he cried, "Yuck! It's in my mouth!"

"Serves you right," said Chase, and got out a pair of nice shiny handcuffs, then launched into his arrest procedure with visible satisfaction.

And as Dudley was hauled off, Odelia asked, "Why did you do it, Dudley?"

Dudley shrugged. "The money, what else? Millions and millions, or so I'd been told."

"Told by who?"

He was still spitting out goo. "Frank Butterwick. I used to work for him, and he knew everything about this mall project. They'd asked him to install a pool on the roof."

Odelia narrowed her eyes at the kid. "So you're Brett? Brett Cragg?"

He grinned. "Now aren't you the clever one… sis."

Odelia glanced at Chase. "Better add one more charge to Brett's charge sheet."

"Yeah, what's that?"

"The murder of Frank Butterwick."

"Oh, the old fool had it coming," said Dudley, proving himself to be anything but the son of Odelia's dad.

And when she thought about all he'd done, Odelia suddenly found herself hauling off and slapping the kid across the face.

Dudley moved his jaw. "I guess I deserved that."

EPILOGUE

"This stuff is great," said Brutus.

"Yeah, amazing," Harriet agreed.

"When did Tex get so good?" asked Dooley.

"One word," I said with a smile. "Catering."

Since Tex wasn't always to be trusted when performing his feats of culinary mastery behind the grill, Marge had decided not to take any chances this time, and had hired a caterer to organize the family's next barbecue.

It wasn't every day, after all, that you survive an attempt on your life, and she wanted to celebrate her new lease on life in style, and without Tex's regular grilling mishaps.

We were all in the backyard, Tex looking a little sad now that he didn't have a pivotal role to play, and the rest of the family looking ecstatic at the quality of the food they were able to sample.

"You know what, Tex?" said Chase as he clapped his future father-in-law on the back. "Why don't you and I take a barbecue course together? That way we can tackle this problem once and for all."

The doctor's face lit up. "You mean that? You would do that for me?"

"Of course! Anything for my dad," said the cop, causing the older man to wince.

"So Dudley confessed, huh?" said Charlene as she sampled some of the dumplings and closed her eyes at the exquisite taste.

"Yeah, he confessed everything," said Uncle Alec, who was tackling a very large steak with relish. "The murder of your uncle, the attempted murders of my entire family, the attack on the cats—the whole enchilada."

"And all for a little bit of money," said Scarlett. "So sad, right?"

"Not a little bit," Charlene corrected her. "Last time I talked to the developers they mentioned some pretty big numbers. Too bad the deal fell through."

"Maybe it's all for the best," said Marge, who looked happy and healthy again. "Money seems to bring out the worst in people, as we have all been able to witness firsthand."

"Money would have bought me a nice new car," grumbled Gran, who was picking at a piece of fish filet. "A nice Escalade for the watch."

"How is your Gofundme going, Gran?" asked Odelia.

"Oh, don't ask," said Gran. "So far we only got one donation. Ten bucks. Ten bucks won't buy me a new car."

"If you want I can get you a good deal on a secondhand police cruiser," said Uncle Alec.

"No, thanks," said Gran. "The watch isn't going to drive around in an old cop car. We're going to stand on our own two feet, showing everyone we're just as good at catching criminals as you cops are."

"Suit yourself," said Uncle Alec with a shrug, and squirted a goodish helping of tartar sauce on his steak.

Clarice, who was also lying on the porch swing, now yawned and said, "I think I'll get going, you guys. All this hominess and coziness is making me antsy."

"See ya, Clarice," I said.

"Thanks again for saving our lives," said Harriet.

Clarice held up a paw in response, then wandered off.

Rambo, who was lying at our feet, opened a lazy eye. "Oh, is Clarice going already?"

"Yeah, she's got things to do and cats to see," I said with a smile.

"If it hadn't been for her instructions, I would never have gotten you out of that couch," said Rambo.

Clarice had said she returned when she got a bad feeling about this whole Dudley business, and figured she might as well give Odelia another chance—which was very nice of her. And very… compassionate, which had become Harriet's favorite new word.

"Look, I think we should suggest to Odelia that she adopt Clarice," said Harriet now. "I mean, it's the *compassionate* thing to do, right?"

See what I mean?

"Clarice will never do it," said Brutus. "She's an independent soul and doesn't want to be tied down."

"Maybe if we ask her nicely?"

"She won't do it, I'm telling you."

"Maybe if you ask her?"

"Me? Why me?"

"Because she likes you, Brutus. I've seen the way she looks at you."

"I'm sure that's all in your head, sweet peach."

"No, it's not. A cat knows these things."

"Just your imagination."

"Oh, Brutus, don't you deny that you like her, too. I've seen how you look at her."

"I don't look at Clarice!" said Brutus with a light laugh.

"Yes, you do. Just admit it!"

"I'm not admitting anything!"

"Because it's true!"

And as Harriet and Brutus jumped off the swing, to pursue their 'compassionate' conversation elsewhere, I heaved a sigh of relief. I like Harriet and Brutus, I really do, but sometimes a cat just wants to have a little peace and quiet.

And I'd just closed my eyes for a nap, when Dooley said, "Max?"

"Mh?"

"So Dudley wasn't really Tex's son, right?"

"No, he wasn't. Just pretending to be his son so he could pocket those mall millions."

"So… why did Tex believe he was his son?"

"Because Dudley claimed that one of Tex's old girlfriends was his mother." This was the reason Dudley had been going through Tex's old photo albums: looking for an old girlfriend he could believably cast in the role of his mother. And the reason he tried to kill us was because Frank Butterwick had mentioned some of the rumors surrounding Odelia's cats: that we acted as our human's unofficial guards. So he figured he'd better get rid of us before we could cause him any trouble, just the way he tried to get rid of the entire Poole family, figuring those millions would end up in his pocket that way.

Okay, so Dudley was a killer—I never said he was a clever killer, though.

And of course he'd gotten rid of Charlene's uncle because he was the only person in town who knew him under his real name. And he would have spoiled his big plan.

"So… maybe this so-called mom of Dudley—this Jaqlyn Checkers—really did get pregnant? And maybe she really did have a son or daughter whose dad is Tex?"

I looked up at this. "You really think so?"

Dooley shrugged. "Tex believed it. So something must have happened back then to make Dudley's story so plausible."

We both looked out across the backyard at Odelia's dad, who now sat chatting happily with Chase about the barbecue course they were going to take together.

I shook my head. "I really hope no more kids come crawling out of the woodwork."

"I'm just saying, Max."

"I know, buddy. And maybe you're right."

"Humans are always full of surprises, aren't they?"

"Oh, yes, they are."

And as we both glanced at Odelia, we wondered how she would react if Tex's real son suddenly showed up on our doorstep. I had a feeling she'd welcome him with open arms, because that's the kind of person she is. That's the kind of people all the Pooles are. And that's probably why I like them so much.

They're good people, and sometimes bad people try to take advantage of them. But that's what they've got us for, right?

To keep an eye on them.

To be their watchcats.

Because watching out for our humans is what we do.

"Max?" asked Rambo.

"Mh?"

"I'm hungry."

I smiled. "Of course you are."

"Can you ask Odelia for more food?"

"Absolutely, buddy."

In fact we don't just watch out for our humans, we even watch out for our humans' dogs. Now how weird is that?

"Thanks," said Rambo when Odelia dropped a pork chop between his front paws.

She patted his head. "You know?" she said. "Maybe we'll adopt you."

Wait… "What?!"

"Chase is always going on about having a dog, so let's adopt Rambo," she said.

"I wouldn't mind," said Rambo with a casual shrug. "As long as the food's good? Sure."

Odelia must have noticed how Dooley and I were staring at her, absolutely flabbergasted, and she grinned. "Don't look at me like that, you guys. It'll be fun. And you like Rambo, don't you? Sure you do."

And with these words, she returned to her family, still grinning, and proving once and for all that humans don't understand the first thing about cats. Nothing!

"Max?" said Dooley.

"Yes, Dooley?"

"Let's elope."

"Why not?" I said, and hopped down from that swing.

"We can live off our urine," said Dooley as we walked off and left that treacherous and very uncompassionate Poole family behind. "Just like Gandhi. It's a self-fulfilling prophecy: you drink the pee, then you pee, then you drink the pee, then you pee, and then you drink the pee, and so on and so on."

"That's not a self-fulfilling prophecy, Dooley."

"A pee-petuum mobile, then?"

"Oh, Dooley," I said.

EXCERPT FROM PURRFECT FOOL
(THE MYSTERIES OF MAX 28)

Chapter One

It could have been the perfect nap. The nap to end all naps. Unfortunately there was one thing that detracted from absolute perfection. Or I should probably say one bug: a big, fat fly kept buzzing around my head, making it impossible to enjoy the full benefit of my slumber.

I'd already given this fly the evil eye, but the darn thing didn't seem to be all that quick on the uptake, and just kept at it. Giving it the cold shoulder didn't help either, and so finally I saw no other recourse than to swat at the annoying thing, making my displeasure known not only in word but also in deed.

"Hey, cool your jets, bro!" said the fly, and buzzed off to rob some other pet of sleep.

And so I finally closed my eyes to pick up where I left off when something else intruded upon my much-yearned-for peace and quiet.

Gran came stalking in through the sliding glass door and

slammed a newspaper down right next to me, then proceeded to take a seat—unbidden, I might add.

"Will you look at that!" she exclaimed, causing me to suppress a groan of annoyance and direct a casual glance at said newspaper.

"What is it?" I asked, not in the mood for reading an entire newspaper article and preferring to get the gist straight from the horse's mouth—in this case my human's gran.

"It's that no-good son of mine," the old lady announced, clearly not all that happy with whatever that son of hers had been up to this time. For those of you not in the know, Gran's son is none other than Alec Lip, chief of police in our neck of the woods.

"What did he do?" I asked, more out of politeness and the faint but diminishing hope that this would speed up the process of getting Gran to take her leave and leave me to my hopes and dreams of that catnap I'd been looking so forward to.

"He says he's going to get married! Married, if you please!"

I yawned. "Isn't that a good thing?"

"Not in the same year my granddaughter is tying the knot it isn't!" said Gran. She poked a finger at the newspaper, causing it to crumple. "He's stealing Odelia's thunder, that's what he's doing! How dare he!"

"So maybe you can organize a double wedding? Would save you time and money."

"A double wedding!" Gran cried, clearly aghast at the prospect. "Never in my life will I attend this wedding. Never, you hear me!"

"I hear you," I said, wincing a little, for Gran was even more voluble than usual.

Dooley, who'd been attracted by all the hullabaloo, came

prancing over from the pantry, where he'd done his business in his litter box. I could tell he'd done number two, for he had that distinct spring in his step and that merry gleam in his eye he gets when successfully managing to exorcise the product of his mastication and digestion process.

"What's going on?" he asked when he saw Gran's unhappy face. "Did someone die?"

"No, but someone soon will," said Gran with a dark frown at the newspaper.

"Oh, no!" said Dooley, his face falling. "I didn't even know you were sick, Gran. Is it cancer? Or old age?"

Gran gave my best friend a withering look that would have made a more discerning cat wince. "I'm not dying. And for your information, I'm not old. It's my son."

"Oh, no! Does Uncle Alec have cancer?"

"Nobody has cancer!" she cried. "He's getting married!"

Dooley gave me a look of confusion. Usually when humans get married it's cause for cheer, the prospect of a party making everyone happy. But Gran seemed to liken the occasion to a funeral, which was a novel way of looking at the sacred institution.

"Oh, I get it," said Dooley. "Uncle Alec is sick and dying and he wants to get married before he dies." He shook his head sadly. "I liked Uncle Alec. I'll be sad when he's gone."

"Please talk some sense into your friend, Max," said Gran. "I don't have the patience."

"Uncle Alec isn't dying, Dooley," I explained. "He's getting married, and Gran isn't happy about it."

"But why?" asked Dooley, an understandable question. But then his face cleared. "Oh, I know! Charlene is pregnant! And Uncle Alec doesn't want her to have the baby out of wedlock. Just like in that Lifetime movie we saw last week, when Derek the company boss had to marry his secretary Francine when she announced she was pregnant, only she wasn't pregnant, and only said she was so he would marry her. And then when he found out she wasn't pregnant after all, he immediately had the wedding annulled."

Gran gave Dooley a pointed look. "You know, Dooley, that's something that hadn't occurred to me. But you're right. It's the only possible explanation. Charlene must be expecting a baby. Why else would they suddenly announce their wedding plans?"

"Or it could be that Charlene is dying of cancer," Dooley suggested. "And Uncle Alec wants her to die as his wife."

The prospect of her son's betrothed dying a slow and painful death seemed to please Gran, but then she shook her head. "Nah. He would have told me if she was sick." She shrugged. "Which means I'm going to be a grandma soon."

"But… aren't you a grandma already, Gran?" asked Dooley.

"I hope it's a boy," said Gran, ignoring Dooley. "Or twins. A boy and a girl, maybe."

Dooley gave me a look of supreme worry. For some reason he has this idea that if a newborn enters our family, they'll get rid of all the cats. And no matter how many times I've assured him this is simply not the case, he keeps coming back to the horrifying notion.

"Anyway," said Gran, getting up and grabbing her newspaper. "Just thought I'd let you know. I can't tell the rest of the family how I feel about this wedding nonsense, so I hope you'll keep your mouths shut. Not a word to Alec, you hear? Or the others, for that matter."

"My lips are sealed, Gran," I said.

"Your lips look fine to me, Max," said Dooley, studying my lips intently.

"It's just an expression, Dooley," I said. "It means I won't tell anyone what Gran just told us."

"That goes for you, too, Dooley," said Gran. "If word gets

out that the groom's mom opposes the wedding, there will be hell to pay."

And with these words, she stomped off again, her face a thundercloud.

Somehow I had the feeling it wouldn't be long before the entire town of Hampton Cove would know exactly how Gran felt about the wedding. We might be able to keep our mouths shut, but would Gran?

Chapter Two

"So... let me get this straight," said Dooley. "Uncle Alec is getting married to his girlfriend because she's dying? Or because *he's* dying? Or because she's pregnant?"

"I have no idea, Dooley," I said, still holding out a faint hope to have that nap.

"Or maybe Charlene is dying *and* she's pregnant!" His furry face fell. "I hope she'll be able to deliver the baby before she dies, Max."

"I'm sure that Uncle Alec and Charlene are simply getting married because they love each other," I said. "And that there is no pregnancy and that no one is dying."

"Or it could be that Uncle Alec is pregnant," said Dooley, my reassurances landing on deaf ears as usual. "He looks like he's pregnant, with that very big belly of his."

"Uncle Alec is pregnant?!" suddenly a cry sounded from the kitchen. I looked up and saw that Harriet and Brutus had arrived, the other two cats that make up our household.

Brutus is a butch black cat, and also Harriet's boyfriend, who's a white Persian. They both looked flabbergasted by this piece of news.

"Uncle Alec can't be pregnant," I said with a laugh. "Men don't get pregnant, you guys."

"I wouldn't be too sure about that, Max," said Brutus.

"Nowadays everybody can get pregnant."

"He's right," said Dooley. "I saw a documentary on the Discovery Channel the other night about a man who delivered a healthy baby boy."

"So let me get this straight," said Harriet. "Uncle Alec is pregnant… with a boy?"

I heaved a deep sigh. I had a feeling I wasn't going to get any naptime anytime soon with this lot launching into a discussion on my human's uncle being pregnant.

"As I understand it now," said Dooley, "Uncle Alec is pregnant, and his future wife Charlene is also pregnant, *and* dying, which is why they're tying the knot in a hurry."

Harriet's eye went a little wider. "Uncle Alec and Charlene are getting married?"

"Yeah, looks like it," I said. At least that part of the story was undoubtedly true.

"But… he can't get married!" said Harriet. "Odelia and Chase are getting married. Uncle Alec can't steal her thunder —it's just not fair!"

"Exactly what Gran said," I agreed, nodding. I watched that fat fly flit hither and thither, and was already yearning for the good old days when it had been just me and it.

"We have to do something about this, you guys!" said Harriet, getting all worked up now. "We can't let this wedding take place!"

"It has to take place," said Dooley. "Because Charlene and Uncle Alec are both dying, and they're both pregnant, too, so they have to get married before it's too late."

"Dooley!" said Harriet. "Are you serious?!"

I felt it was time to intervene before things got completely out of hand. "Look, the only thing we know for sure is that a wedding has been announced and will be taking place between Uncle Alec and Charlene," I said. "The rest is just idle speculation."

"But—" said Dooley.

"Idle speculation," I repeated emphatically.

As I'd expected, my words acted like oil on the raging waters of Harriet's indignation and Dooley's rampant imagination, and for a few moments a pleasant silence reigned.

Then Dooley said, "Maybe Odelia is pregnant, too, and very soon she'll kick us all out, because everybody knows that cats and babies don't mix, so there's that to consider."

"Oh, Dooley," I said, and that big fly, which had taken advantage of me being distracted by landing on the tip of my nose, said, "If you want, I can go and find out for you, cat."

And I said, "Wait, what?"

The fly shrugged and said, "Haven't you ever heard the expression 'Fly on the wall' before? Well, I can be that fly for you, cat."

So I said, "Sure. Why not?"

Anything to get rid of this fly. Now if only I could get rid of my housemates, but somehow I had a feeling this wasn't in the cards.

Chapter Three

The life of a fly is often a pretty lonely life—and a short one, too. So Norm, as he buzzed off on his mission, was actually happy with this change of scenery. His brethren and sistren might content themselves by eating dirt, but Norm was that rare fly who had, from the moment he was born, entertained higher aspirations. He'd always envisioned himself as that rare breed of fly: the adventurous type. And overhearing those cats speculating about their humans, Norm had smelled an opportunity and grabbed it.

So first he buzzed off in the direction of the house next door, where that old woman had disappeared to, and decided to pick up some little tidbits of raw intelligence there, just like James Bond would, if James Bond was about half an inch in diameter and consisted of an exceedingly hairy body, six hairy legs, two compound eyes and some extra-sensitive antennae. Though in all honesty all that Norm had in common with James Bond was a hairy chest and that can-do attitude your average British spy has in spades.

And he was in luck, as Grandma Muffin had just grabbed her purse and was on her way out the door, so he simply followed in her wake, hoping it would lead to something.

He landed on top of her head, before being rudely swatted away—the life of a fly consists mainly of being swatted away—and ducked into her car just as she did.

"Stupid fly," Grandma Muffin muttered as she gave Norm one of her trademark dark looks, then started up the engine, and floored the accelerator, causing the car to lurch away from the curb at a much higher rate of speed than traffic cops like to see.

Moments later, it seemed, they were already cruising through downtown Hampton Cove, and when the older lady steered her car into an underground parking garage, Norm was buzzing with anticipatory glee. Looked like he was in for a real treat!

Maybe a meeting with some Deep Throat type informant? A showdown in the bowels of what looked like a boutique hotel? He didn't know what would follow, but had a feeling it was going to be good. So it was with a slight sense of disappointment that he watched Grandma Muffin simply park her car, get out and slam the door then walk off.

They took the elevator up to the hotel lobby, and once again Norm's hopes soared: a secret meeting in one of the hotel rooms with a foreign spy? A dead drop in one of the hotel's garbage bins of some secret documents? So when the old lady Max called 'Gran' met up with a gorgeous redhead with plunging décolletage in the hotel lobby, and the both of them walked into the dining area, he knew this was it. The redhead was probably a Russian spy, here to hand over the secrets to the Russian rocket program, or maybe even spike Grandma's drink with a little-known nerve agent or truth serum!

So when both women took a seat in the outside dining area and ordered drinks from a suspicious-looking waiter—a Korean spy? A Chinese double agent?—he was on the lookout for the little vial containing the deadly nerve agent, and ready to warn Gran!

"We gotta do something, Scarlett," said Gran. "We have got to stop this wedding."

"But why?" said the woman named Scarlett, tossing her red curls across her shoulders. She was dressed in a provocatively cleavaged red dress and red high heels, her lips a very bright Scarlett and looking every bit the sexy Russian secret agent.

"Why? Are you kidding me? They're going to ruin Odelia's wedding!"

"I think it's pretty cute. And you can always make it a double wedding," said Scarlett, taking a sip from her drink—a flat white, if Norm had followed the proceedings closely. So far no little vials with deadly nerve agents were in evidence but that could happen any moment now.

"Trust me on this, Scarlett. Alec wouldn't be getting married if he wasn't being coerced—if Charlene wasn't putting a knife to his throat." She slapped the table, causing her own drink—hot cocoa with plenty of cream, from the looks of it—to dance up and down. "That woman's got something on my son and I want to know what it is."

"Isn't it possible that they simply love each other and want to celebrate that love by tying the knot?" asked Scarlett, who was clearly a romantically inclined Russian spy.

"Oh, Scarlett, Scarlett," said Gran. "I see she's gotten to you, too."

"Nobody's 'gotten' to me, Vesta. I just think they make a damn fine couple, and I wish them all the future happiness in the world, and frankly I think you should, too."

"He's too old to get married!"

"He's only, what, fifty-something?"

"I'm telling you Alec would never get married if he wasn't being hoodwinked. And I want to know what that woman is holding over him."

Scarlett shrugged. "Can only be one thing."

Vesta gave her a scathing look. "You've got a one-track mind, Scarlett."

"What? I'm telling you—in my experience there's only one thing that would make a man want to propose marriage to a woman and that's—"

"Don't say it. Don't you dare say it."

"Sex! What else?"

"I'm the man's mother, Scarlett!"

"So? There are certain realities you just have to face, Vesta. Charlene is an attractive woman, and I'm sure she's got assets that would make any man happy to explore them."

Gran buried her face in her hands. "Oh, God."

"It's human nature!"

"Just because you're obsessed with sex doesn't mean we all are."

"Just saying," said Scarlett with a shrug.

Norm was losing his patience. So far nothing was happening that would make James Bond bother to get out of bed in the morning, and he was starting to wonder if Max had sent him on a fool's errand. He wouldn't put it past the cat to try and get rid of him.

"Look, I want to find out what Charlene's got on my son, and then I want to stop that wedding from happening.

Are you with me or not, that's all I need to know right now."

"Well…" said Scarlett, wavering.

"It's going to break my granddaughter's heart, Scarlett! And I happen to love my granddaughter—more than anything in the world!"

"Aww," said Scarlett, regarding her friend with interest.

"What's the look for?"

"So you do have a heart."

"Of course I have a heart!" She then wagged a finger in her friend's face. "But don't you go and blab about it. It would ruin my reputation."

"Okay, fine. I'll help you. What do you want me to do?"

"First we need to find out Charlene's secret."

"And how do you propose we do that?"

"Easy. We spy on her."

"What do you mean?"

"We bug her phone, her house, her office, we put a tracker on her car…"

"Isn't that, like, extremely illegal?"

"Who cares? I'm trying to protect my family here, Scarlett!"

"Fine! But aren't you forgetting one thing?"

"What?"

"We're not exactly professional spies, you and me. So how do you propose we pull this off?"

Grandma Muffin smiled. "Leave that to me. I've got it all figured out."

Okay, so it wasn't exactly the high-profile spy bonanza Norm had anticipated, but he still felt, as he started the long flight back to Harrington Street to report to Max, that he'd gleaned some interesting intelligence. And he was starting to see that he'd landed himself in exactly the kind of spy story Mr. Bond would have appreciated.

ABOUT NIC

Nic has a background in political science and before being struck by the writing bug worked odd jobs around the world (including but not limited to massage therapist in Mexico, gardener in Italy, restaurant manager in India, and Berlitz teacher in Belgium).

When he's not writing he enjoys curling up with a good (comic) book, watching British crime dramas, French comedies or Nancy Meyers movies, sampling pastry (apple cake!), pasta and chocolate (preferably the dark variety), twisting himself into a pretzel doing morning yoga, going for a run, and spoiling his big red tomcat Tommy.

He lives with his wife (and aforementioned cat) in a small village smack dab in the middle of absolutely nowhere and is probably writing his next 'Mysteries of Max' book right now.

www.nicsaint.com

ALSO BY NIC SAINT

The Mysteries of Max
Purrfect Murder
Purrfectly Deadly
Purrfect Revenge
Purrfect Heat
Purrfect Crime
Purrfect Rivalry
Purrfect Peril
Purrfect Secret
Purrfect Alibi
Purrfect Obsession
Purrfect Betrayal
Purrfectly Clueless
Purrfectly Royal
Purrfect Cut
Purrfect Trap
Purrfectly Hidden
Purrfect Kill
Purrfect Boy Toy
Purrfectly Dogged
Purrfectly Dead
Purrfect Saint
Purrfect Advice
Purrfect Cover
Purrfect Patsy

Purrfect Son
Purrfect Fool
Purrfect Fitness

Box Set 1 (Books 1-3)
Box Set 2 (Books 4-6)
Box Set 3 (Books 7-9)
Box Set 4 (Books 10-12)
Box Set 5 (Books 13-15)
Box Set 6 (Books 16-18)
Box Set 7 (Books 19-21)
Box Set 8 (Books 22-24)

Purrfect Santa
Purrfectly Flealess

Nora Steel
Murder Retreat

The Kellys
Murder Motel
Death in Suburbia

Emily Stone
Murder at the Art Class

Washington & Jefferson
First Shot

Alice Whitehouse
Spooky Times

Spooky Trills

Spooky End

Spooky Spells

Ghosts of London

Between a Ghost and a Spooky Place

Public Ghost Number One

Ghost Save the Queen

Box Set 1 (Books 1-3)

A Tale of Two Harrys

Ghost of Girlband Past

Ghostlier Things

Charleneland

Deadly Ride

Final Ride

Neighborhood Witch Committee

Witchy Start

Witchy Worries

Witchy Wishes

Saffron Diffley

Crime and Retribution

Vice and Verdict

Felonies and Penalties (Saffron Diffley Short 1)

The B-Team

Once Upon a Spy

Tate-à-Tate

Enemy of the Tates

Ghosts vs. Spies

The Ghost Who Came in from the Cold

Witchy Fingers

Witchy Trouble

Witchy Hexations

Witchy Possessions

Witchy Riches

Box Set 1 (Books 1-4)

The Mysteries of Bell & Whitehouse

One Spoonful of Trouble

Two Scoops of Murder

Three Shots of Disaster

Box Set 1 (Books 1-3)

A Twist of Wraith

A Touch of Ghost

A Clash of Spooks

Box Set 2 (Books 4-6)

The Stuffing of Nightmares

A Breath of Dead Air

An Act of Hodd

Box Set 3 (Books 7-9)

A Game of Dons

Standalone Novels

When in Bruges

The Whiskered Spy

ThrillFix

Homejacking

The Eighth Billionaire

The Wrong Woman